Praise for Kate Hoffmann's Mighty Quinns

"Keep your fan handy! It was impossible for me to
put this steamy, sexy book down
until the last page was turned."
—*Fresh Fiction* on *The Mighty Quinns: Jack*

"This truly delightful tale packs in the heat
and a lot of heart at the same time."
—*RT Book Reviews* on *The Mighty Quinns: Dermot*

"This is a fast read that is hard to tear the eyes from.
Once I picked it up I couldn't put it down."
—*Fresh Fiction* on *The Mighty Quinns: Dermot*

"A story that not only pulled me in,
but left me weak in the knees."
—*Seriously Reviewed* on *The Mighty Quinns: Riley*

"Sexy, heartwarming and romantic, this is a story to
settle down with and enjoy—and then reread."
—*RT Book Reviews* on *The Mighty Quinns: Teague*

"Sexy Irish folklore and intrigue
weave throughout this steamy tale."
—*RT Book Reviews* on *The Mighty Quinns: Kellan*

"The only drawback to this story
is that it's far too short!"
—*Fresh Fiction* on *The Mighty Quinns: Kellan*

"Strong, imperfect but lovable characters,
an interesting setting and great sensuality."
—*RT Book Reviews* on *The Mighty Quinns: Brody*

Dear Reader,

It's hard to believe I'm finishing up another set of
Quinn books. This series was really fun to write and I
spent more than a few hours wondering what I'd do
if some distant relative left me a million dollars. Not
too much time, though, since I know I don't have any
wealthy relatives out there.

Though I've had a chance to give away a lot of
Aileen Quinn's money, I think there might be a
little more left in the bank account. Who knows
what Quinns might be found in the future?
The Mighty Quinns: Dex is my twenty-sixth story
about the family. I think there might be a few more
stories left to be told. Stay tuned!

Best,

Kate Hoffmann

The Mighty Quinns: Dex

Kate Hoffmann

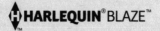

ISBN-13: 978-0-373-79781-3

THE MIGHTY QUINNS: DEX

Copyright © 2013 by Peggy A. Hoffmann

Printed in U.S.A.

ABOUT THE AUTHOR

Kate Hoffmann began writing for Harlequin in 1993. Since then, she's published nearly eighty books, primarily in the Temptation and Blaze lines. When she isn't writing, she enjoys music, theater and musical theater. She is active working with high school students in the performing arts. She lives in southeastern Wisconsin with her cat, Chloe.

Books by Kate Hoffmann

Prologue

"THE HOUSE LOOKS lovely, Sally. Just lovely."

Aileen Quinn stood in the foyer of her Irish country house and gazed around at the festive holiday decorations. Though the first week in November was a bit early to put everything up for Christmas, she didn't care.

Most people waited for the Feast of the Immaculate Conception on December 8 before bringing out the decorations. But this year, optimism filled her with the holiday spirit. This year, for the first time in her memory, she'd spend the holidays with almost her entire family, and she wanted to savor that joy for as long as possible.

"It does look grand," Sally said. "I've missed all the holiday cheer." The housekeeper slipped her arm through Aileen's and smiled at her. "I believe this will be our best Christmas ever."

"I was thinking we ought to put another tree upstairs," Aileen said. "Just at the top of the stairs. We still have my collection of German glass ornaments, and they would fill a small tree."

In years past, she'd made up for her lack of family by overdecorating the house, hoping that it might fill her with more Christmas spirit. But it had never worked. No matter how beautiful the decor, she had still been alone. So for the past twenty years, she'd just stopped, not bothering to acknowledge the holidays at all. It had been too painful, bringing up so many regrets.

The doorbell chimed and Sally left her side. "I suppose that will be Mr. Stephens." She peeked out the door, then turned back to Aileen. "And he's brought a guest. A young lady."

Aileen's eyebrow arched up and a smile twitched at the corners of her mouth. "Well, now, isn't that a surprise? The last time I spoke with Ian, we discussed his rather dismal social life. I can't believe he acted so quickly."

Sally pulled the door open. Grasping her cane, Aileen moved to greet her guests. Her gaze fell on a pretty young woman with bright green eyes and dark hair that fell in soft waves around her face. "Hello there," Aileen said, holding out her hand. "I'm Aileen Quinn."

Two spots of color rose in the woman's cheeks and she smiled. "Miss Quinn, it is such a pleasure to meet you. And thank you for welcoming me into your home." She glanced around. "It's just beautiful."

By the accent, Aileen could tell the young lady was American. Aileen looked over at Ian. "Would you care to make the introductions, Mr. Stephens?"

"Ah, yes, yes. My apologies. Miss Quinn, this is Marlena Jenner from Back Bay Productions in Boston. She's the producer I told you about. The one who wants to make a documentary about your life."

Aileen chuckled softly. "I see. Well, Mr. Stephens, I admire your persistence. But as I said before, I'm not certain my life would be so interesting on film."

"Oh, but I disagree," Marlena said. "Yours is a rags-to-riches story. And your books are so popular worldwide that I'm sure all your fans would want to get to know you better. You've done so few interviews over the years, Miss Quinn." She drew a quick breath, then quickly continued on. "And Ian has told me about your search for your brothers. Perhaps this documentary could help to find Conal." She turned to Ian. "It is Conal, right?"

He nodded and forced a smile as she started to continue with her plea. But Aileen jumped in. "Miss Jenner, I—"

"Please, call me Marlie. We're going to be working closely over the next few months, after all. At least I hope we are. I'm your biggest fan. I've read all your books. Some of them three or four times. They got me through a very difficult point in my life."

Aileen glanced back and forth between Ian and Marlie. "Well, I suppose if you're that determined, then we ought to sit down and talk. Sally, would you get us tea? We'll have it in the library."

Aileen started off in the direction of the library, then looked over her shoulder to find Marlie standing mute in the hallway, an expression of shock on her face. Starstruck—because she'd invited her to tea? "Come along, then."

Maybe the pretty young woman was right. This might be the only way to find Conal and his heirs. A film about her life and her search for Conal and her other lost siblings would go much further than her autobiography ever would.

She didn't have much time left to finish her search. At ninety-seven, she was grateful for every sunrise she saw. And she was busy planning a huge family reunion over the Christmas holidays, renting a castle and making arrangements for a wonderful time for all.

But it wouldn't be complete without knowing what had happened to Conal. The clues to his existence, and any possible heirs, were out there somewhere, waiting for her to find them. And if she wasn't willing to do absolutely everything to make that happen, then why bother with her search at all?

She waited for Marlena to catch up to her, then slipped her hand around the younger woman's arm. "So tell me, Miss Jenner. How will this all work? When will we begin?"

"Next week," Marlie said. "We'll begin filming interviews with you, and we'll finish by filming your new family at your holiday celebration, if they agree."

The young lady seemed quite invested in this project. And she was a fan, so Aileen could count on the film being complimentary. She had nothing to lose and everything to gain. Conal. He was the only one still missing.

"Lovely," Aileen said. "And how quickly will your documentary be finished?"

1

HE WOKE in a cold sweat, the darkness in the room swallowing him like a giant black vortex. Dex Kennedy gasped for breath, sitting up and throwing aside the covers on the bed.

His bare chest was damp with perspiration, yet the room had a chill. Where was he? What time was it? He drew a deep breath, searching for a scent that might give him a clue. He wasn't in the desert; he wasn't in the jungle. The smell of lavender clung to the sheets, and he realized he was in Ireland, in his sister's flat in Killarney. There was no danger. He was safe.

Dex turned on the bedside lamp, then rubbed his eyes with the heels of his hands. When would the nightmares end? he wondered. It had been nearly a year now, and though his body had healed from the two gunshot wounds, his mind was still back on that landing strip cut out of the jungle in Colombia.

He and his filmmaking partner, writer and director, Matt Crenshaw, had gone there to get footage for a documentary about the drug wars that had plagued the country. With help from some locals, they had managed to film damning footage of one of the most powerful cartels. They were almost to the plane and to safety when the cartel's thugs had pinned them down with automatic weapons fire from the surrounding bush.

Matt had been hit in the leg before they were able to get on the plane and make their escape. Hit in the femoral artery, Matt had bled out in front of Dex, a couple thousand feet above the jungles of southern Colombia.

It had all happened so fast. Matt had been alive and cracking jokes one moment and gone the next.

Dex drew another ragged breath and ran his fingers through his hair. A bottle of sleeping pills sat unopened on the bedside table. Maybe he ought to give in and take a few. The prospect of sleeping an entire night was almost too much to resist. He wanted to lose himself in that feeling of utter exhaustion again, to finally let his mind rest.

Dex reached for the bottle. Twisting open the cap, he dumped the pills into his hand and stared down at them. He could understand why someone might just toss back the whole lot of them. Sleep deprivation could do queer things to the mind, make you take desperate measures for just a few moments of peace.

Cursing beneath his breath, he hurled the pills at the wall and they scattered around the room.

"Dex?" The muffled sound of his sister's voice came through the door. "Are you still awake?"

"Yeah," he called.

"Are…are you all right, then?"

"Fine," Dex said. He swung his legs off the bed and stood up, searching for the battered trousers he'd discarded earlier. The bloodstains were still there, but they had faded over the past months. Dex pulled them on, leaving the top button undone.

He ought to have thrown the trousers out. They were a constant reminder of what had happened. But Dex wanted to be reminded. Matt had been his best friend and the only partner he ever wanted to work with. Running his palm over the stain, Dex felt emotion tighten his chest. He wasn't going to forget.

His twin sister, Claire, was standing outside the bedroom door, a worried expression on her face. Her cropped dark hair was standing up in unruly spikes and her face, usually made up with red lips and dark eyeliner, was freshly scrubbed.

"You look feckin' awful," she murmured as he walked past her. "Really, Dex. How long are you going to carry on like this before you get some help?"

"I went round to the chemist and picked up some sleeping pills," Dex muttered, heading for the kitchen.

"Didn't they work?" Claire asked.

"I didn't take them."

She threw up her hands. "Well, that's probably why they didn't work, then. You just have to get back into a routine and a few good nights' sleep."

Dex grabbed a bottle of beer from the refrigerator and returned to the living room, snatching up the remote for the telly and switching on the twenty-four-hour sports station.

Claire plopped down beside him on the sofa, her hands folded on her lap. She stared at him silently, and when he glanced over at her, he saw tears of frustration in her eyes and a tremble in her bottom lip. "Don't," he murmured. "I'll be all right. It's just going to take some time."

"Maybe you should find something to do with yourself," Claire suggested. "Hanging around my flat like some out-of-work bowsie isn't doing you any good."

"What do you propose I do? I've been a filmmaker since I was fourteen. It's all I've ever wanted to be. I'm not sure I'm suited to sell cars or work the bar in a pub."

"That's not what I meant. I've peeked at your mobile. Your agent has all sorts of projects he's been texting you about. I've been taking calls, too. Why don't you just talk to these people? See what they have for you? It couldn't hurt."

Dex took another swig of his beer. He shouldn't be surprised by her snooping. There had never been any secrets between them. "It wouldn't be the same. I was a decent cameraman, but Matt was the one who made the stories work. I can tell a story with pictures, but I can't do it with words. He had all the talent in the partnership."

Claire grabbed a scrap of paper from a nearby table and held it out to him. "Ian Stephens. I've taken three messages from him. A lovely man, by the way, with a very sexy English accent. He sounds like James frickin' Bond. His number is right there, along with the number of the woman he's working with, Marlena Jenner. She's the producer on the project."

He stared at the two numbers. "What is the project? Did you ask?"

"It's a film about Aileen Quinn."

"The writer?"

Clare nodded. "My favorite writer. Ireland's favorite writer."

"That's not the kind of work I do."

"That might be a good thing. At least no one would be shooting at you."

"I'm not ready to go back to work," he said.

"But you just said it, Dex. It's who you are."

"Hell, I'm not sure who I am anymore," Dex whispered, his voice filling with emotion. "I—I just don't know what I want." He shook his head. "Wait, I do know. I know exactly what I want—to sleep through the night. That's my fondest wish."

Claire put her arm around his shoulders and they sat next to each other for a long while. This was the way it had always been between them. They had weathered tough times in the past, but they'd always had each other to lean on.

Their parents had lived a gypsy life, both of them actors who'd garnered a fair bit of success in Ireland's small film industry. As a family, they'd lived in London, New York City, Toronto and then Dublin again. But when his father had been cast in an American television series, they'd all moved to California, an Irish family living amongst the movie stars and palm trees and the constant sunny weather.

It had been a difficult transition for Dex and Claire, at that point already in junior high, and they hadn't made friends easily, preferring to spend time with each other. So when the series had been picked up for its fourth season and Claire and Dex were ready to enter high school, they decided to return to County Kerry and live with their father's mother, a woman they affectionately called Nana Dee.

Dierdre O'Meara Kennedy had seen them through their teenage years, then sent them off to university— Dex to film school at UCLA and Claire to read history at Trinity in Dublin. Nana Dee had provided the only stable home they'd ever really had, and her little cottage on the Iveragh Peninsula was the place they'd always called home. Nana had passed away three years ago, and had left them her cottage filled with memories of her life.

"There is something you could do for me," Claire said.

"I'm not going to help you mark your history exams," he said. "Or untangle the mess you've made of your laptop. Or fix that banger of a car you drive."

"We still have to clean out Nana's house," she said. "I know you considered staying there while you were home, but you've spent every night here. So I thought we could lease the cottage out. But to do that we have to go through everything and decide what we want to keep and what we'd like to donate to the parish for their tag sale."

"She lived in that house for over fifty years," Dex said.

"I know. But I trust you to go through it. It will occupy your mind," she said. "And we could really use the extra money. My pittance as a history teacher won't support your taste for beer and whiskey much longer." Claire grabbed the bottle and took a long swig before handing it back to him. "Don't misunderstand, I'm glad you're here. But you're starting to look a little pale and paunchy. You need to go outside. Get some sun and exercise."

Dex chuckled. "All right. I suppose I can do that. What do we want to keep?"

"We'll leave the furniture so we can let it out as a furnished cottage. And the clothes, I'll go through. There's probably some vintage stuff that I could wear. Sort out the mementos, the old photos and things, and we'll go through those together."

The idea appealed to Dex. He needed to focus his mind on something other than his lack of a plan for the future. Maybe if he exhausted himself with cleaning out his nana's house, he'd finally get some sleep—and some perspective.

"Actually, I have someone who wants to look at the place tomorrow," Claire said. "She's going to be an exchange teacher at our school next term. Just show her around the cottage and tell her it will be all tidied up before she moves in in January."

"I suppose I can do that, too," he said.

Claire rested her head on his shoulder. "Good. Would you like me to make some popcorn? I've got the next series of *Dr. Who* ready to go. We could stay up and watch it."

"It's half past two," Dex said.

"And it's a Friday night. I don't have to work tomorrow. We can stay up all night if you want to."

"All right," Dex said. "But I'll make the popcorn. You never put enough butter on it."

Claire laughed, then wrapped her arms around him and gave him a fierce hug. "Things will get better, baby brother. I promise they will."

He smiled. He'd been born only six minutes after her, but she'd always called him her baby brother. "Yeah. I know they will," Dex said.

Yet even as the words passed his lips, he didn't believe there was any truth to them. His life, as he once knew it, was over. And now he was adrift in a dark sea of indecision. Things would never be the same. How could they be?

MARLENA JENNER STARED down at the road map and then looked at the signpost in front of her. Maybe she ought to just give up and ask for directions. It was nearly dark and she'd never find her way once she couldn't see the road signs. There was no shame in admitting that she couldn't navigate her way out of a paper bag. And it seemed as if she'd been driving around in circles for hours.

Crumpling the map up and tossing it aside, Marlie shook her head. "Just let it go," she said. "Ireland is an island. And I'm on a peninsula. Sooner or later, I'll find the place or I'll run into water."

"Knockaunnaglashy," she muttered, reading the road sign. "Where do they find the names for these towns?" She put the Fiat into gear and started down the narrow road. After leaving numerous messages with Dex Kennedy's agent and receiving an equal number of promises that he'd get back to her, she'd almost given up and moved to the next guy on her list. But then, to her surprise, she'd received a call from Dex Kennedy's sister, Claire, who had told her exactly where to find Dex.

When it came to Irish documentary filmmakers, Dex Kennedy was the best. Word was that he was between jobs, recovering from the loss of his friend and partner, Matt Crenshaw, and looking for just the right project. And Marlie had the perfect project for him.

Sure, it wasn't the kind of high-stakes, action-packed story that he usually did, but that didn't mean it wasn't important. And she'd found a wonderful angle to the story that she hoped might intrigue him.

"What's the worst he can say?" she murmured to herself. "No?" She'd heard that word plenty of times. And she'd learned that when someone said no, you simply had to find a good enough reason for them to say yes. This reason was definitely good enough.

Thanks to her grandmother, she'd finally put together the funding to do a documentary on her all-time favorite author, Aileen Quinn. And Aileen had agreed to participate. They were scheduled to start filming in five days. A filmmaker of Dex Kennedy's caliber and reputation would legitimize the project to the industry.

With the help of Quinn's researcher, Ian Stephens, and with Dex Kennedy as her coproducer, they'd create something that celebrated Miss Quinn's long and colorful career and make a film that would be shown all over the world—maybe even at Cannes or Sundance. She would have proved herself as a producer. No one would be able to doubt her then.

But first she had to find Dex Kennedy. The road wound down a long hill and suddenly the directions made sense. "Turn right at the blue cottage with the thatched roof," she repeated, "and drive until the bushes come over the car." She bumped along on a rutted road for what seemed like forever, and just as she was ready to turn back, she saw a long line of bushes arched over the lane. "Make another right at the stone wall next to the old abbey." And again, the wall and a ruined abbey appeared.

Marlie smiled. Maybe she'd been a little harsh on herself. Claire Kennedy's directions had been spot-on, once she'd actually figured out where she was.

The landscape offered a beautiful view of rolling hills crisscrossed by dry stone walls and the sea beyond. Like every spot in Ireland, the green of the hills here was so vivid that it nearly hurt her eyes to look at it. Perhaps it was the sun, which seemed to hang lower in the sky, always shining from behind fluffy white clouds. Marlie wondered if the landscape would look as beautiful onscreen as it did to her eyes.

She saw the sign for the village before she saw the small gathering of cottages and outbuildings. Though she was only a half hour outside Killarney, this seemed like a place out of another time.

There were no numbers on the cottages, but Claire's description of the place was enough to locate it. She pulled up in front of an overgrown privet hedge and got out of the Fiat. The front garden was unkempt, the summer perennials now faded in the early-November chill.

Marlie drew a deep breath and started up the stone walk, running over her sales pitch in her head. She hoped to appeal to his sense of national pride. Who better to film this documentary about a great Irish writer than a great Irish filmmaker? He was the best person to tell this story. And it would be a nice change of pace for him, give him a chance to sleep in his own bed.

Marlie bit back a groan. Was that even a factor for a guy like Dex Kennedy? He'd been to Sierra Leone and Chechnya, Libya and Afghanistan, living in primitive conditions to get the best stories. He probably didn't worry about creature comforts....

Marlie rapped sharply on the front door. A few seconds later, it swung open. Her breath caught in her throat as a tall man stared at her in curiosity. His shirt was unbuttoned down the front, revealing a smooth expanse of skin and muscle. And his raven hair, shaggy and thick, was tousled around his face, as if he'd just crawled out of bed.

All she could manage for a greeting was a pathetic squeak. "Hi," she said.

"Hello," he replied. His gaze fixed on hers and his brow furrowed. Marlie urged herself to state her case as quickly as she could before he tossed her out. But for the life of her, she couldn't think about anything but how incredibly handsome Dex Kennedy was in real life.

She'd seen photos, but they just hadn't done him justice, as he'd usually been wearing sunglasses and a cap pulled low over his eyes—the silent partner in the pair. He'd always managed to make himself seem very mysterious…and a little dangerous, too. But now, without cap or sunglasses, she realized he had striking features, high cheekbones and a perfectly straight nose, a strong chin and lips that were…very kissable. She swallowed hard. He was, most definitely, the kind of man who made a girl's knees weak and her heart pound.

Marlie searched for a flaw in his face and had almost given up when she noticed the dark smudges beneath his eyes. He looked as if he'd been out late the night before. Marlie wondered if lack of sleep might make him more irritable and less likely to listen to her proposal. She decided to proceed carefully.

"My sister mentioned you'd be calling," he said, stepping aside. "Come on in, then. I'm Dex. Dex Kennedy."

Oh, that accent. If his looks hadn't unnerved her, then his voice would finish the job. Deep and rich, each word lilted with the sound of Ireland. She thought she'd grown used to it over the past few weeks, but obviously she hadn't.

"And you might be?" he asked. "I'm sorry, I'm afraid I've forgotten if my sister told me your name."

"Marlie. Marlie Jenner," she said.

Well, this was off to a good start, she thought. He hadn't slammed the door in her face. Maybe Claire had decided to pave the way for her.

"Come on," he said.

Marlie realized she'd been frozen on the front step.

She picked up her foot to move, concentrating on projecting a confident air. "Thank you," she said.

"It's a bit chilly in here," he said. "We've been keeping the temperature down to save on heating costs. Let me show you the kitchen. It's this way. Tea?"

Marlie followed him, not sure what there was to see in the kitchen or why it seemed so important to him to show her. Though her job really didn't include fixing tea, she was willing to make quite a few concessions to get Dex to agree to her project. Besides, making tea might give her a little more time to collect her composure.

"I could make you some tea," she offered.

"Only if you'd like some," he said.

"Actually, I prefer coffee."

"Would you like coffee?"

"No," Marlie said.

An uncomfortable silence grew between them. Maybe she was a little starstruck. After all, this was Dex Kennedy, award-winning filmmaker. And he was hot.

"What do you think?" Dex finally said.

"About?"

"I know, it's not a very posh setup. But everything works, it's just a little old. You have your cooker and your oven. There's no microwave and not many modern conveniences. I guess some people might find it charming."

"Yes. It is that."

"I suppose you'll want to see the bedrooms?" Once again, his gaze met hers, but this time it lingered just a little longer than necessary. Was he feeling the same strange attraction as she was? Or was this all in her overactive imagination?

"They're this way," he finally said, leading her back out into the living room. She walked behind him, taking the chance to admire the muscular shoulders beneath the faded cotton shirt. Her attention dropped lower and focused on his backside…just as he suddenly stopped and turned around.

His brow rose and she thought she saw a tiny twitch of a smile at the corners of his mouth. "Go right in," he murmured. "Do you want to test out the mattress?"

Marlie's heart slammed in her chest. Was this some kind of game he was playing, trying to shake her confidence? Or was it a test to see just how far she'd go to get what she wanted? Though it wouldn't be difficult to fall into bed with this man.

"Mr. Kennedy, I think—"

"It's not a big bed," he said, pointing to it inside the bedroom door. "But I think there would be plenty of room for…whatever." He nodded. "Go on, then."

With a trembling hand, she opened the bedroom door and walked inside. What the hell was going on? "Mr. Kennedy, I'm not sure that—"

"You don't have to call me Mr. Kennedy," he said, his voice soft as he stood behind her. "Dex will do."

Marlie pressed her hand to her chest, her heart pounding beneath her fingers. This was crazy! She didn't even know this man, and yet, if he'd just give her a tiny little push, she'd fall onto the bed, ready to let him…ravish her.

"Ah…"

"Dex," he said, as if she needed a reminder.

In truth, for a moment there, she *had* forgotten his name—and the reason she'd come. "Dex," she repeated. Slowly, she turned, determined to face her fears.

"Oh, and Claire says the rent is very reasonable," he said. "For a place like this."

"Rent?"

"You didn't think you'd be paying rent?"

"Did your sister tell you I was coming?"

"Yes. She said you'd be needing a place to stay next term. While you're here teaching."

Ah, obviously, he thought she was someone else. But maybe she could use that to her advantage. Considering the rather uncanny skill he had of avoiding her until now, she wasn't about to give him a chance to toss her out on her ear. If they could just get to know each other, maybe he'd be more inclined to accept her proposal.

"What is the rent?" she asked.

"Didn't Claire tell you?"

Marlie shook her head. "I think she wanted to make sure I liked what I saw first." She glanced up and met his eyes.

"And do you?" he asked, his gaze fixed on hers.

His attention drifted to her lips and Marlie held her breath, wondering if he was contemplating something more than just conversation. A man didn't just stare at a woman's mouth for no reason. Unless, of course, she had something in her teeth. Oh, God.

"I do," Marlie said. "Where's the bathroom?"

He pointed to a door near the entrance to the kitchen and she hurried over and stepped inside. Staring into the mirror, she smiled, examining her teeth. No, nothing. Marlie groaned inwardly. That meant he was staring at her mouth because he—

"Is there anything else I can show you?" he asked, appearing in the doorway.

She quickly spun around, leaning back against the sink. All right, he *was* toying with her. Maybe it was time to put a stop to this and tell him why she was really here. Marlie drew a steadying breath.

"Would you like to get something to drink?" he asked. "Or maybe something to eat? Dinner, perhaps?"

"I—I had a late—a late lunch," she stammered, unable to fashion a quick answer. Was he asking her out? Or was he just hungry? "But I could eat," she added quickly.

"Good. There's a pub just down the road. The food is good." He smiled. "Great. Let's go, then."

He buttoned up his shirt and grabbed his jacket, then held the door open for her. When she got outside, Marlie offered to drive, but Dex insisted they take his SUV, a dusty BMW. He opened the door for her and helped her inside. Marlie watched him through the front window as he strode around to the driver's side. It still felt odd sitting on the wrong side of the car, driving on the wrong side of the road. But everything about this day seemed a little upside-down and backward.

For now, she'd just roll with it. What harm could it do? She needed him. And when the time was right to tell him exactly who she was, she'd tell him.

"Ready?" he asked as he slid in behind the wheel. Marlie nodded. "I think so."

THE PUB WAS quiet when they walked in. Dex held the door open and Marlie stepped in front of him. He clenched and unclenched his fingers, fighting the urge to place his hand in the small of her back.

For the first time in a very long while, he wasn't dwelling on the past. No, he was firmly in the present, his mind racing and his body reacting. She was so pretty, though not really the kind of girl he was usually attracted to. He normally went for the more exotic beauties, French and Italian women, certainly not some American girl-next-door type. But then, he wasn't the same guy anymore. Maybe his preferences had changed.

They found a table near the bar, and Dex held out her chair as she sat down. He took a place across the table, offering himself a better vantage point to study her. The barkeep appeared a few moments later with menus. He ordered a Guinness and Marlie did the same.

"When in Ireland," she said before taking a sip.

He stared at her mouth as she licked the foam off her lips. There'd been quite a few moments in the past hour when he'd lost himself just looking at her. She was like a breath of fresh air, blowing all the cobwebs out of his head and making his body feel alive again. But was he really interested in seducing this woman? She was a teacher. And Claire's coworker. But, hell, if she was willing, then who was he to refuse pursuing the matter? There was an obvious attraction between them, and he was used to acting quickly when it came to sex. He was never in one place more than a night or two, which didn't leave a lot of time for foreplay.

"My sister says you're going to teach at her school next term. What do you teach?"

"Uh…that's boring. Tell me about yourself," she countered. "You're a filmmaker."

He frowned. "How did you know that?"

"I've seen your films," she said.

Dex sat back, crossing his arms over his chest. Though he knew he had fans, he rarely met them, except when he was accepting some kind of award.

"I was sorry to hear about your partner," Marlie added. "That must have been such a dark time for you."

Until that moment, he'd put the nightmare out of his head. But now he realized that would never be completely possible. "It was," he said. "But I'm trying to focus on other things now."

"That's a good philosophy," she said with an encouraging smile. "What's your next project?"

If only she knew, he thought to himself. Screw filmmaking; his mind was occupied with plans for a full-on seduction. "I'm considering my options," he said.

"I have an option for you," Marlie said.

Unless it had to do with tearing her clothes off and having at it right here in the pub, Dex really wasn't interested. But he had the luxury to take things slow. "I don't want to talk about work," he countered. "Let's talk about what you're doing tomorrow. The term doesn't start until after the New Year. Are you going back to the States for Christmas? What about your family? Don't they celebrate together?"

"They do. But I'm usually working and can't get away and I—"

"You work over Christmas in the States?" he asked. "You don't have a school holiday?"

She looked at him, her eyes wide, then cleared her throat. "I'm not a teacher," she said. "And I'm not interested in renting your cottage, although is a very nice place."

Dex stared at her for a long moment, taking in the look of confusion—no, desperation—on her pretty face. "I don't get it," he said.

"My name is Marlena Jenner and I'm working on a documentary film about Aileen Quinn. I've been trying to track you down through your agent, and when he wasn't getting any response, I decided to take matters into my own hands. Your sister, Claire, said—"

"Marlena. Right. You're the not the teacher." Dex quickly stood. She'd been playing him. He bit back a curse. He'd told both his agent and his sister that he wasn't even going to think about work for at least another year. He needed a damn break, and he didn't appreciate that his sister had sent this woman to try to change his mind.

"You know, I'm really not interested," he said.

"But you haven't heard about the project yet," Marlie said, following him to the door. "I'm sure once you—"

He spun around to face her, his anger bubbling over. "Listen to me," he said. "I'm not interested." He shook his head, then walked back to the bar and tossed enough money on the polished surface to cover their drinks.

What the hell was happening to him? He could usually read people better than this. He should have seen that she had some ulterior motive. But the moment he set eyes on her, all he could think about was getting her into bed. Not that that feeling wasn't still with him. But no-strings sex didn't work unless they were both interested in the same outcome—pure lust and mutual sexual satisfaction. She was just playing along until she could pitch him her idea.

He strode outside, Marlie hard on his heels. "Wait," she said. "Just give me a chance to explain."

He yanked the passenger door open. "Get in. I'll take you back."

"No," Marlie said.

Dex gasped. Was she really going to draw a line? He couldn't exactly leave her standing in the middle of the road. It was at least a fifteen-minute walk in the cold, windy night to get back to her car. And he wasn't the type of guy who'd leave a woman stranded.

Dex slammed the door. "All right. If you want to pitch your project, go ahead. Right now."

Jaysus, she was beautiful. Her color was high and her green eyes bright. And her hair whipped around her face in windblown strands. He wanted to reach out and grab her, twist his fingers through the thick mass of waves and pull her into a very long kiss.

She shifted nervously, then stared down at her toes. "I left my laptop in my car. The pitch is better with visuals. I have a whole presentation made up."

With a low chuckle, he pulled the door open again. "Let's go, then."

Reluctantly, she got inside. When he joined her, she turned in her seat and faced him. "I didn't mean to mislead you. I just thought if you got to know me, you might trust me a little more."

"Oh, sure. Lying is always the best way to get a bloke to trust you."

"Can we just start over?" Marlie asked. She held out her hand. "Hi, I'm Marlena Jenner. I'm a producer at Back Bay Productions in Boston. I'd like to talk to you about making a documentary about the Irish author Aileen Quinn." When he didn't reciprocate, she wiggled her fingers. "Come on. It goes both ways."

Dex laughed and took her hand. "Really? And what did I do to mislead you?" She opened her mouth, then snapped it shut, yanking her fingers away. Dex gave her a dubious look. "What?"

"You wanted to kiss me," she said, tipping her chin up defiantly.

"I did not." God, was he that transparent? Usually he was much more discreet about his desires. "Where did you get that idea?"

"I can just tell," she said.

"Oh, really. How? From your vast knowledge about men? Irish men, in particular?"

She sat back in the seat and crossed her arms over her chest. "You don't know anything about me," she said.

"And you know next to nothing about me," he countered.

"I know what you want."

"Prove it."

What happened next happened so quickly that Dex wasn't able to stop it. In one quick movement, she leaned over, grabbed his face between her hands and kissed him. At first, he wasn't sure what to do, but then he took advantage of the invitation and slipped his hands around her waist, pulling her closer.

Her lips parted slightly and he slipped his tongue into the sweet warmth of her mouth. When a tiny sigh slipped from her throat, Dex took it as another invitation and dragged her body on top of his until he could run his hands over her backside. His pulse pounded, the warmth of desire pumping through his body.

The kiss ended as quickly as it began when Marlie drew back and looked at him with a wide-eyed gaze. "I—I think I've made my point." She scrambled over to her side of the SUV and quickly fastened her seat belt. "We can go now," she murmured.

"Bloody hell, you must really want me to do this project."

"I do," she said. "It's imperative."

"Imperative?"

"Yes, no one else could do it like you could." She drew a sharp breath. "I mean the documentary," she quickly added. "Not the kiss." Marlie cleared her throat. "But the kiss was good, too."

"Yeah, that's what I thought you meant." He started the truck, his heart slamming in his chest. He'd never reacted so strongly to a simple kiss.

"Just so you know, that's not usually part of my pitch. Nothing is going quite the way I intended."

"Will there be more kissing involved, or is it all business from here on out?"

"Would kissing you make you more inclined to take the job?" she asked.

"Probably not," he replied.

"Then I suppose that's the last time I'm going to kiss you."

"Good," he said, throwing the truck into gear and pulling out onto the road.

Though Marlie Jenner would provide the perfect distraction from all the pain he'd experienced in the past eight months, he wasn't about to use her just to satisfy his own lust. He wasn't ready to work again, and nothing she offered him, even a few enjoyable kisses, was going to change his mind. Once he got her back to the cottage, he'd send her on her way.

2

MARLIE USED THE ride back from the pub to silently go over her pitch in her head. She'd have just one chance to convince him, and she had to make sure she got it right.

Dex pulled the SUV onto the small parking pad next to the cottage and turned off the lights, then the ignition.

"I'll just go get my computer," she murmured, reaching for the door.

But he placed a hand on her arm, stopping her. "Wait," he said.

Her gaze drifted down to the spot where his fingers rested. A warm flush crept up her cheeks and she had to tell herself to breathe. "What is it?"

"I have to be honest with you. As much as I enjoyed that kiss we shared, nothing you say is going to convince me to do your project. So I don't need to see your presentation. But if you'd like to come inside and get to know each other a little better over a drink, I'd be interested in that."

Marlie stared at him, her mouth agape. "I— How dare—? No! No, I'm not interested in coming inside and having a drink." She opened the car door and stepped out, then slammed the door.

Dex jumped out after her. "I just thought since you *did* kiss me and you seemed to enjoy it that…"

Marlie shook her head, then turned to walk away. In truth, she wanted nothing more than to go inside with him and see exactly where a few drinks might lead. But that would be supremely unprofessional. Plus, she didn't want to give him the satisfaction.

She spun back around. "You're missing out on a really great project. You have a chance to do something important for a wonderful Irish writer. And don't think I don't know you could do this project blindfolded with one hand tied behind your back."

Dex smiled. "That would be a bit dodgy," he said.

Marlie cursed beneath her breath, then strode toward her car, fighting back the tears that threatened. She'd blown it. And yet, as she got inside her car, she couldn't put her finger on where she'd gone wrong. Somewhere between the pub and the cottage, he'd changed his mind. Before that, everything had been going so well.

Or had it? Maybe he'd never had any intention of listening to her pitch. Maybe all he really wanted was a quick roll in the hay. She grabbed the keys from her jacket pocket and started the car. "I never should have kissed him," Marlie muttered.

She'd never been an impulsive person, especially

when it came to men. There was just something about Dex that rendered her completely irrational.

Throwing the car into gear, she steered the Fiat back onto the road, roaring past Dex as she headed toward the lights of the village.

As she drove through the dark, she refocused, scrambling to come up with an alternate plan. But Marlie was faced with the realization that she'd put all her eggs in the Dex basket. Though she had a list of other options, other cameramen who might be interested in the project, she hadn't made contact with any of them. She'd never expected to waste two full weeks chasing after Dex Kennedy, and filming was due to start in mere days.

Rain began to hit the windshield and she turned on the wipers. When she reached the small village, Marlie pulled the car over and grabbed the map, trying to figure out the fastest way back to Killarney. Yet the thought of walking away from Dex and everything he had to offer was causing her to doubt her actions. She'd come this far. Was she really ready to give up so easily?

"No," Marlie muttered. He hadn't even given her a chance. She cursed softly. At least not a chance to talk about her project.

So just how far was she willing to go to convince Dex to do her film? She'd never compromised herself for the sake of professional advancement. Yet now that the film of her career was about to slip through her fingers, she had to take drastic action, and she wasn't going to give up. Not until she'd exhausted every last option with Dex. Every last option, except sex. That, she decided, was her line.

Marlie made a quick U-turn and headed back toward the little cottage. When she reached the building, she pulled up near the stone wall and turned off the ignition.

The house was dark and she wondered if he'd left already. But the SUV was still parked in its spot. It was early, not even 8:00 p.m. Had he gone to bed? If she waited here, she could catch him in the morning, maybe in a better mood. Or she could bang on the door and demand that he hear her out.

Marlie grabbed her laptop and got out of the car. Nothing had ever come easily to her. Why would Dex Kennedy be any different? Somehow, she would put aside her ridiculous attraction to him and keep her wits about her. And she'd convince him that this film was the most important thing in her life—and his.

When she reached the door, Marlie drew a deep breath. "He's just a guy. Just an ordinary guy. He's not that good-looking. Or charming." She rapped on the door, her heart pounding. After a second knock, Marlie realized he wasn't planning to answer.

"I know you're in there. I'm not going away until you give me a chance to pitch my project."

Marlie put her ear up against the door. But she heard nothing inside. "I'm not going to give up. You can talk to me now, or you can talk to me later."

She reached for the doorknob. Holding her breath, she slowly turned it, surprised when the door opened. The last thing she needed was to be accused of breaking and entering. But since the door was unlocked, she couldn't be accused of breaking in, and if she stayed on the front step, she wouldn't be entering.

"Hello?" The interior was dark, the only light coming from the remains of a fire in the hearth. "Dex? Are you here?"

If he was going to be this stubborn, then maybe she'd need to be a bit more aggressive. Besides, he wouldn't call the police, would he? "I'm not breaking and entering, I just have a few more things I want to say."

She switched on a lamp and then walked slowly through the cottage. But Dex was nowhere to be found. Maybe he'd gone out for a walk.

It was cold and rainy outside. He'd have to come home sooner or later. She'd wait in the car until she saw the lights come on, and then she'd knock again.

Marlie walked back out to her car and crawled inside, pulling her jacket around her to ward off the chill. He couldn't stay out that long in weather like this… unless a friend had picked him up and they'd gone out. She groaned. He could be gone until the pubs closed.

Her cell phone rang and she pulled it out of her pocket. "Hello?"

"Miss Jenner, this is Ian Stephens."

Marlie suppressed another groan. What else was going to go wrong? With her luck, Aileen Quinn was probably having second thoughts, too. "Hello. How are you?"

"I'm fine. I hope I'm not ringing too late, but I wanted to let you know that I got all of Miss Quinn's photos on a disk. You can pick them up tomorrow or I can drop them at your hotel."

"If you could drop them off, that would be great," Marlie said. "I'm a little busy with other matters."

"And Miss Quinn has asked if we could move the first interview forward one day. She had a conflict come up. And I think she's excited to get started."

"Yes," Marlie said. "That would be fine. So we'll be there Friday instead of Saturday."

"That will do. Have a pleasant evening and I'll see you soon."

Marlie hung up and slipped the phone into her pocket. She leaned back and closed her eyes. She had to make this work. She'd already told her bosses at Back Bay she could get Dex Kennedy to sign on to the project, and they'd already begun making plans based on her overly optimistic claim.

How could she go back to them and tell them she'd failed? They'd lose all faith in her. They already had their doubts. There was only one choice—she'd have to convince him, no matter what it took.

THE DAMP WIND stung his cheeks and Dex shoved his hands farther into his pockets. He was chilled to the bone but he didn't feel the cold. All he wanted was the numbness that it brought.

The moon had come out from behind the clouds, illuminating the wet road in front of him. He knew this route so well in the dark, navigating from cottage to cottage by the light spilling out of the windows.

The weather matched his mood—foul and dark.

He'd paced the cottage for a full ten minutes, regretting his decision to send Marlie Jenner away. Then the walls had begun to close in and he had to escape.

If he walked long enough and fast enough, he'd exhaust himself and maybe get a little sleep. His encounter with Marlie certainly hadn't done anything to relax him. After her reaction to his invitation for a drink, he realized the mistake he'd made. He'd assumed the attraction was mutual, but she'd obviously only been flirting with him in the hopes it might help her cause. He'd misread her interest.

He'd been so long without a woman that he couldn't even read the signs anymore. In eight months, he hadn't even considered indulging in the pleasure of a woman's company. And now, suddenly, he was desperate for another chance to touch her, to lose himself in the taste of her mouth or the scent of her hair.

Because in that single moment when their lips had met, he'd felt as if a door had been thrown open and the sun had shone through with blinding white light that had warmed his soul. He'd sensed his life might finally get back on track, if he could just spend a little time standing in that light.

What was it about her that he found so alluring? She was pretty, that much was evident. He couldn't take his eyes off her face. But there was something else that drew him to her. She had an innocence, a naïveté, that he usually didn't find in the women he dated.

How easy would it be to fall into a relationship with her, and for all the wrong reasons? She was just like that bottle of sleeping pills, a drug that made all his problems disappear, a drug he'd soon come to crave, knowing all the while that he was just medicating the problem, not solving it.

Then there was the matter of professional ethics. He'd never mixed his personal life with his professional life. It was a strict rule that he and Matt had made for themselves and it was part of the reason they had been so successful. When they were immersed in a project, there were never any distractions.

And if that wasn't reason enough, Dex couldn't drag her into his messy life. No one, not even someone as tempting as her, deserved that. He'd done the right thing in sending her away. He needed more time to heal.

But how much more? Dex wondered. When would he start to feel this darkness lift? There were days when he could barely crawl out of bed.

And yet the moment he'd set eyes on Marlie, all of that had been forgotten. So maybe he just needed a woman, any woman, to distract him for a bit. Any woman except Marlie Jenner.

As he neared the cottage, Dex noticed a car parked on the road just outside the garden gate. He squinted in the darkness, trying to make out who it might be. Had Claire decided to drive out and keep him company? The moon emerged again and he made out the silhouette of Marlie's Fiat.

"Bloody hell," he muttered. As he approached the car, he wondered if she'd decided to wait inside. But the cottage was dark, just as he'd left it.

He peered into the window and saw Marlie, curled

up in the front seat, her eyes closed. Dex rapped softly
on the window and she jerked, startled by the sound.
As she looked out at him, he circled his finger, silently
asking her to roll the window down.

"What are you doing out here?" he demanded.

"Waiting for you," Marlie said, rubbing her eyes
and sending him a weak smile.

"I thought we'd settled everything earlier."

"You didn't let me make my presentation," she
snapped. "I'm not going to let you say no until you've
listened to what I have to say."

Dex circled around the car, but instead of going
back inside the cottage, he waited for her to unlock
the passenger-side door. When she did, he got inside,
settling himself into the seat.

He rubbed his hands together to warm them. "It's
not that I wouldn't like to work with you," Dex murmured. "I just don't think I'd be any good to anyone
right now. I've sort of lost my focus and I'm not sure
I'm going to get it back."

"You won't know unless you try," Marlie said.

"I know that I just spent three hours in the rain trying to get you out of my head."

She drew a sharp breath and glanced away, rattled
by his declaration. "Maybe you're feeling guilty that
you didn't give me a chance?"

Dex chuckled. "What I'm feeling has nothing to
do with guilt." He twisted around in the small seat
and faced her. "Tell me, why are you so determined
to make this film? Beyond fame and fortune, which
I can promise you, you won't find making documen-

tary films. So there must be a reason. Why this film? Why Aileen Quinn?"

She considered his question for a moment, as if she wanted to make sure she gave him the answer he was seeking.

"Don't tell me what you think I want to hear," he warned. "Tell me the truth."

She nodded. "When I was younger, I was…lost. I didn't really fit in—with my family, with the kids in school. I felt like an outsider most of the time. Then one day, I picked up one of Aileen Quinn's books at the library. I think I was twelve, and I was so excited that the librarian had given me an adult book. I found myself in that book. The heroine in the story was all alone in the world, but she was so strong and determined, nothing could stop her. And in the end, she made a wonderful life for herself. And I told myself that I could do the same thing." Marlie met his gaze. "Aileen Quinn changed my life. I know that sounds dramatic, but it's true."

"That's a good reason," he murmured. "You're passionate about your subject."

"So maybe instead of thinking of all the reasons why you can't do this project, you should think about the reasons why you should."

"And what might those be?" Dex asked.

"I'll be honest. With your name attached to the project, it's going to get much more attention than it ever would with just my name. People will be interested in seeing it. We'll get distribution and interest at the film festivals."

Dex turned away, letting the sound of her voice lure him back in again. Everything she said was true. His name would open a lot of doors for her. And it wasn't as if he was doing anything useful with his time, beyond lying around Claire's flat and drinking far too much.

But if he did agree to do the film, he'd have to maintain the same professionalism he and Matt had insisted on. He'd have to find a way to keep his mind—and his hands—off Marlie.

"There are other guys in Ireland who could do the job," Dex said.

"But I want you."

He took in the stubborn set of her jaw, the determined look in her eyes, and he felt his resistance softening. The least he could do is listen to her proposal. How the hell was he supposed to say no? Maybe if he found the pitch interesting, he might consider doing the film. But if he found himself more intrigued by the woman than the project, he'd send her on her way.

After all, working might be good for him. But falling into an affair with a beautiful yet vulnerable American had disaster written all over it. And Dex had had enough of disaster lately.

"Tell me something," Dex said. "If I hadn't come along, were you planning on sleeping out here?"

"I guess I was," Marlie said. She shrugged. "I had to give it one more try." She met his gaze. "Will you listen?"

"Yeah," Dex said. "I can't promise you anything, except—" he paused "—except that I'm not going to kiss you again. If we're considering working together, we need to make sure we can keep things professional."

"Of course. There will be no more kissing," she said. "Or touching. Because that could lead to kissing. Strictly professional."

"All right," Dex said. "Why don't you grab your computer and come inside?"

"Now? You don't want to leave this until the morning?"

"No," Dex said. "I'm not tired. We can do it now."

A smile broke across her face. "All right. Thank you. You won't be disappointed. You're going to say yes. I just know it."

As Dex got out of the car, he realized that her prediction was probably right. He'd have a hard time saying no to a woman as beautiful and passionate as Marlie Jenner. She could ask him to strip naked and run down Grafton Street in Dublin and he'd probably do it. So if she decided to kiss him again, how was he going to stop her?

She joined him at the gate, her laptop clutched in her arms. When he opened the front door, he reached inside, flipping on a light. Marlie followed him, smiling brightly.

"I really do appreciate this chance."

Dex helped her out of her jacket, his fingers brushing against her shoulders and tangling for a moment in her hair. The contact sent a current of desire racing through him, and he fought against the reaction.

"I'm going to get a drink," Dex said. "Can I get you anything?"

"What do you have?" Marlie asked. "Something to warm me up would be good."

"Whiskey," Dex murmured. "We need whiskey. Why don't you sit down on the sofa. I'll get the drinks, start a fire and then we'll see what you have to say."

Dex wandered back to the kitchen and grabbed the bottle of whiskey from the cupboard above the sink. He took a long swallow, letting the alcohol burn a path down his throat and warm his body. "Get a grip. She's just a girl. Just a pretty girl."

"So WHAT DO you think?" Marlie grabbed her glass of whiskey and took a slip. "Please tell me you at least find this interesting. I want your creative input. I—I realize it's not the kind of project you usually do. But it's a wonderful story, and she's an incredible woman. You're going to love her and—"

Dex pressed a finger to her lips and Marlie stopped. She'd made her pitch. Now it was time to let him do the talking. So she asked, "Do you have any questions? Or comments, maybe?"

He chuckled. "I have a lot of questions. But I'm not sure I should ask them."

"No, I want you to. Challenge me. Argue with me. I want to know exactly what you're thinking."

"You don't have any idea how beautiful you are, do you?" Dex shook his head and groaned. "That's exactly what I was thinking."

"That's not what I meant."

"I know. But it had to be said." He turned her laptop toward him and stared at the old photo of Aileen Quinn.

Marlie watched him as he contemplated his decision. Watching the firelight dance over his face, she wanted to reach out and touch him, to lose herself in the wild sensations of desire and need that had raced through her when they'd kissed.

She couldn't imagine they'd be able to go back to a professional relationship after that kiss, wasn't even sure she wanted to. It had been quite a while since she'd had a man in her life. And she'd never been with a man quite as accomplished—and sexy—as Dex.

But if he felt that a professional relationship was required, she'd do her best to keep her distance.

"Miss Quinn is an interesting subject," Dex said, "but I just don't see a hook here. We'd just be making a filmed version of her biography."

Marlie had held back the most interesting part of the story, hoping it might push him over the edge if he had any doubts. "Aileen Quinn had four older brothers. Shortly after she was born, her mother sent them off to different corners of the world, some with new families. Aileen just learned about her brothers last year and she's been tracking down their descendants. They're all gathering here in Ireland at Christmas for a big reunion, and we're going to be there to talk to them. She's still looking for one of the brothers, Conal, so that search will be part of the film, too. Maybe we'll even find him." She paused. "I was planning on using the search to structure the narrative."

"That does make for an interesting story," he admitted.

"And each of the heirs is getting a million dollars," she said. "Give or take. It's like winning the lottery. It's changed their lives. And there are so many great stories to tell."

He closed her laptop and rested his hand over it. "I have one big concern, though, and that's your obvious admiration for Aileen Quinn."

"I do admire her."

"You have to maintain a proper distance from your subject so that you can see her objectively, warts and all. I won't do this if you're just looking to do a pretty story. You might have to make some tough choices, and I need to know that you'll be able to do that when the time comes."

Marlie shifted uneasily. "I'm not sure I understand what you mean."

"No one lives a perfect life, Marlie. And if you're going to tell Aileen Quinn's story, you need to tell the good parts along with the bad ones."

"There are no bad parts," Marlie said. "I've read her autobiography. She's led an exemplary life."

"Everyone has skeletons in their closet," he said. "Our job is to find them."

"No," Marlie said. "I'm not going to turn this into some exposé."

"I wouldn't, either. I'm simply talking about discovering the truth of her story and making a movie about it. It's all part of the person she is, and *that's* the story we're telling. The complete story. Can you do that?"

Marlie grabbed her laptop. "Yes, of course." She could promise that. She knew that Aileen had lived a scandal-free life. Dex would discover that, and realize there were no skeletons to find.

"All right," Dex said, getting to his feet. "I've got everything I wanted to know. Can I have some time to consider?"

"Sure," Marlie said. "But not long. We're scheduled to start shooting on Friday."

"Friday?"

Marlie nodded. "I know it's soon, but I didn't think it would take this long to track you down and convince you."

"Weren't there any others on your short list?"

"No. Not really."

"Well, if I decide not to do it, I'll help you find someone else."

"I don't want someone else," she said stubbornly. "I want you."

"You've made that very clear," Dex replied.

Marlie glanced at her watch, surprised to see that it was nearly 1:00 a.m. Getting to her feet, she wavered slightly, the effect of too much whiskey suddenly hitting her. "I should go. I've got a long drive back to Killarney."

"You can't drive. You've had too much to drink."

Marlie ran her hands through her hair. "You're right. Maybe I could call a car? A taxi?"

Dex stood and took her hand, then drew her back down onto the sofa. "I think it would be better if you stay here tonight."

"No. I don't have anything with me, and—and we would be asking for trouble." She glanced down at their fingers, now tangled together so tightly that she couldn't distinguish his hand from hers.

"I'd drive you myself, but I've had more to drink than you have. It will be fine. You can stay in one bedroom and I'll stay in the other." He placed her hand on her knee and drew his away. "If we're going to be working together, we're going to need to get used to hanging out together."

"You're going to do it?" Marlie asked, her heart leaping in her chest.

"I can't think of a good reason why I shouldn't. And I can think of one good reason why I should."

"What is that? And please don't say it's because you like to kiss me."

"No, I believe we could make a helluva good film."

Still, Marlie wondered if his reason for accepting her offer had less to do with her proposal than what had happened when their lips met. But if they were going to spend the next few months working on the documentary, then they'd have to trust each other.

"Yes, the film will be wonderful," she said. "So I guess I can have my people call your people and we'll iron out the details of a contract?"

"All right. And tomorrow morning, we'll get started."

"I've put together a production schedule. Since I've already scheduled our first interview with Aileen for Friday, we have a lot of work to do before then. I think you should meet Aileen first so you can get to know her. You're going to love her."

"No, I'm not. And you shouldn't, either," he warned.

Marlie ignored him. It was ridiculous to think that she shouldn't admire Aileen. "And Ian Stephens, her research assistant. He's providing a lot of the background information on the search. I also have a contact who will digitize all the archival photos we want, and I've looked at a few spaces for a temporary studio."

"I have a small studio in Dublin where I store all my equipment. We can use that."

Marlie couldn't believe it had all worked out so well. Earlier that afternoon, she'd thought the film—and her career—was ruined. But tomorrow they'd begin work on the project that would transform her into a real producer. She'd finally gotten her big break, and now that it was here, she couldn't wait to get started.

"All right," Marlie said. A wave of exhaustion came over her and she fought back a yawn. "I should probably turn in. I've been up since 6:00 a.m., and the whiskey is making me sleepy."

Dex stood up and took her hands, guiding her to one of the bedrooms. "If you need anything, just let me know."

"I could use something to sleep in," she said.

"Wait here," he said. He disappeared into the other room and returned with a faded rugby jersey. Dex held it out. "Will this do?"

"That will be fine," she said. Marlie paused, fighting the urge to throw her arms around him and kiss him again. It was the only way she could think to communicate her gratitude. A handshake wouldn't do. In the end, she pushed up on her toes and kissed his cheek. "I'll see you in the morning, Dex."

"Good night, Marlie."

When she closed the bedroom door behind her, Marlie leaned back against it and took a ragged breath. This was all so strange, spending the night under the same roof as a virtual stranger.

Marlie crossed the room and sat down on the edge of the old iron bed. Now that he'd agreed to do the film, she'd thought the pressure might fade a bit. But instead, it had only become worse. If they didn't develop a good working relationship, then the next two months would be very difficult.

But Dex was a strong personality, and she'd have to work hard to make sure he took her ideas about the film seriously. She had less experience as a producer and so much more to lose if this film wasn't good. Her bosses at Back Bay already had high expectations for this documentary, and she needed to deliver. And if she did, maybe she'd finally be able to prove to her family that she'd made the right career choice.

It wasn't easy being a Jenner. Both of her parents were surgeons at the best hospital in Boston, her father also serving as chief of staff. Her four older siblings, two sisters and two brothers, had also opted for careers in the medical field, but only after attending Ivy League colleges and prestigious medical schools. *Boston Magazine* had even done a feature article on the Jenners, calling them Boston's first family of medicine.

Marlie sighed. They'd called her the black sheep of the family. She knew what they all thought, that she was somehow defective since she had no interest in the "family business." She'd always loved art and books and movies and music. She'd played the piano and taken ballet lessons, and yet none of her successes as a child had made a difference because she hadn't skipped a grade or two in school or gotten a perfect score on her college entrance exams.

Why was she still bothering to try? Marlie wondered. They'd never consider her work important. She wasn't saving lives or doing critical research. In their eyes, she'd always be a failure.

"But I'm not," she said as she stripped out of her clothes. She had managed to snag Dex Kennedy, one of the world's best documentary filmmakers, and with him at her side, they'd create something everyone would finally be proud of.

The bedroom was damp and chilly, so she quickly crawled beneath the faded bedcovers, then pulled them up to her chin. But the more she tried to relax, the more her mind kept spinning with everything that had happened that day.

Though she'd occasionally had men in her life, her relationships never lasted very long. She usually ended up with men who wanted a sweet, compliant woman who would put her career on the back burner for them, which she tried very hard to be. She'd turn herself into exactly what they wanted, but eventually the charade would become too much bear.

By the end of the relationship, she would feel as if she'd been playing a part, like an actress losing herself in a role. It had come from her childhood, she'd realized, a childhood spent trying to please her parents and her siblings.

In her life, good things had only come to her when she'd stood up for herself and taken control, when she'd been herself. She'd have to exert that same control now. Self-control, Marlie thought.

She closed her eyes and tried to relax, listening to the sounds of the rainstorm that battered at the windows. She heard Dex move about for a short time, and she wondered if he was going over her idea in his head, already planning what he wanted to film.

Then, after about a half hour, everything went silent. She tried to imagine him in the bedroom next to hers, shirt off—pants off. Maybe even naked. Was he lying awake thinking about the kiss they'd shared?

If she were bold, she'd have the courage to walk into his room, crawl into the bed beside him and let nature take its course. But the impulsive kiss they'd shared had to be the end of her seductive ways. Tomorrow, they'd begin again, but this time as business associates. She'd forget the attraction, or at least pretend to ignore it.

Marlie let her mind drift and her body relax, falling into the space between wakefulness and sleep. Until a shout startled her back to reality. She sat up in bed, confused by what she'd heard. She rubbed her eyes and listened carefully, then heard Dex's voice.

Crawling out of bed, she pulled the faded coverlet around her body and walked to the bedroom door. Marlie rested her hand on the doorknob before opening the door a crack.

Was there someone else in the cottage? Who was he talking to?

"Dex?" she called softly. She stepped into the front parlor to find the lights still on. Dex was lying on the sofa, his eyes closed.

It only took a moment for her to see that he was caught in the middle of a nightmare. He mumbled something beneath his breath, desperate words that made no sense to her, a foreign language that sounded like Spanish. He lashed out with his arm, then growled a low curse.

Marlie wasn't sure what she ought to do. She tiptoed over to him, watching the play of emotion on his face, the anger, the pain. The nightmare refused to loosen its grip, and she bent down next to the sofa and touched him on his shoulder. "Dex?"

His body jerked and an instant later, he threw his arm out again, his elbow coming in contact with her eye. Marlie cried out, startled by his action. She pressed her fingertips to her brow, realizing that she was bleeding. She glanced at Dex to find him staring at her in disbelief.

"Jaysus," he murmured. "Did I hit you?"

"No, no," Marlie said. "It was an accident. You were having a nightmare and I tried to wake you and—"

"I hit you," he said. A long string of curses slipped from his lips and he swung his feet to the floor and slid closer to her on the sofa. "Let me see."

"It's nothing," she said. "Just a little bump. I shouldn't have been leaning so close. You were kind of flailing around."

"Come on, come with me." He gently took her hand and drew her to the bathroom. Once he'd flipped the light on over the sink, he turned to her, examining her eye. "It's just a little cut," he murmured. Dex grabbed a washcloth and ran it under the faucet, then pulled her along to the kitchen to get a handful of ice. He wrapped it in the washcloth and held it up to her brow.

"I'm so sorry," he said, shaking his head. "This is why I shouldn't be around people."

"It was just a nightmare," she said. "It's not a big deal, really."

He forced a smile, then turned and walked out of the bathroom, leaving Marlie to stare at herself in the mirror.

She realized that the wounds Dex had suffered last winter were still fresh, and much closer to the surface than she had ever imagined. She'd bet her entire career on the shiny package that was Dex Kennedy…only to discover that the package was broken on the inside.

3

DEX'S HAND TREMBLED as he searched through the drawer for a box of bandages. This was exactly why he couldn't invite a woman into his bed. It was one thing to deal with the nightmares on his own, but she'd be forced to deal with his demons, as well. He couldn't stop the dreams from coming. And this could very well happen again, only worse.

"It's stopped bleeding," she said.

Dex turned to find Marlie standing in the bathroom doorway. She pulled the washrag away from her forehead. "See? All better."

Dex nodded. "I'm sorry," he said. "I just—I don't know what to say."

"It's all right. Really. You don't have to apologize."

Dex had never in his life physically hurt a woman. The idea that he had done just that to Marlie filled him with disgust. "I need to take a walk," he said.

"No," Marlie countered. "Just sit down here." She crossed to the sofa and sat on it, then patted the cushion beside her. She grabbed the half-empty whiskey bottle from the end table and took a sip, then handed it to him.

"What were you dreaming about?"

"Nothing. I don't know," he said. "I can never really remember once I wake up."

"Do you think it has something to do with what happened in Colombia?"

"I shouldn't have told you about that."

"You didn't have to. I did my research," Marlie said. "I'd heard that you didn't want to work anymore because of it."

"But you obviously didn't believe what you'd heard."

"I had nothing to lose and everything to gain," she said. "I figured it was worth the risk."

"Of getting punched in the eye?"

Marlie smiled, then reached out and took his hand, lacing her fingers through his. "Don't you think that's overstating the situation a bit?"

Dex shrugged his shoulders. "I'm Irish. We tend to embellish our stories for dramatic effect."

"I'd much rather say we were set upon by ruffians and I fought them off to save your honor."

He chuckled, leaning back into the overstuffed chintz cushions and staring at the ceiling. He couldn't look at her anymore. She was just too appealing. "I like that story," he said. "Although I'm not sure I would be worth saving."

"Don't say that," she murmured.

He didn't want to like her so much, but there was no way to stop himself when she was so determined to stick up for him. "Were these large ruffians?"

"Very large," she said. "There were at least six or seven of them."

"And you fought them all off?"

"I'm very quick on my feet," Marlie said. "I happen to be a martial-arts expert."

"Really?"

"No. But I did take ballet lessons when I was a kid."

A long silence grew between them, comfortable, soothing his worries. Maybe it was time to step away from his grief and at least try to live a normal life. The dreams might return again, but if he didn't dwell on the past, they might not.

"I don't feel like sleeping," he said.

"Neither do I."

"Maybe we could go over your production schedule. I have a few ideas and I want to get your thoughts. And we haven't even discussed a budget yet."

She shifted, turning toward him. "All right. Let's get to work, then."

As they went over the details of the Aileen Quinn project, Dex began to realize what a challenge it would be. Most of the films he'd worked on were told in a straightforward journalistic style. Facts were laid out, conclusions were drawn and by the end, everyone understood the difference between the good guys and the bad guys.

But this story would be different. It was a "rags to riches" tale, full of heart and warmth, with a little mystery thrown in. Dex wasn't sure he would be able to tap into it, but it was worth a try. Besides, he wanted to spend more time with Marlie, wanted to see where this all might lead. But most of all, he wanted to heal. And when he was here, sitting next to her, touching her, listening to her voice, he felt more whole than he had in a very long time.

"I mentioned that Ian Stephens gave me the rough draft of her autobiography," she said. "And I think we should go through that first. And then I want to weave the stories about her brothers through the narrative, using it as a little mystery, revealing the discovery of each along the way. I think it will keep the viewers engaged as they try to fit the puzzle pieces together."

"Can I ask you something?"

"Sure," Marlie said.

"Is this the kind of project you usually do? What else have you produced?"

She hesitated, then forced a smile. "Lots of things," Marlie said.

"Like what? You obviously know what I'm all about. I need to know what you're about. I'd like to see some of your other projects." He could see she wasn't anxious to answer his question, and he started to wonder if all of this was some kind of scam. Was she really who she said she was? He cleared his throat. "Is there a project?"

Marlie gasped. "Of course there is. Why would you ask that?"

"I just get the sense that you're not being completely honest with me."

She jumped up from her spot on the sofa and stood over him. "All right, all right. This is my first project as a producer. I've been a production assistant on a couple of films, I came up with this idea for a documentary, I went out and got funding for it and here I am."

"Why would someone give a novice funding?" he asked.

"Well, actually, I got the funding from my grandmother. She runs our family's charitable foundation and she's kind of rich." Marlie cleared her throat. "Okay, really rich. But she believes in the project and she wanted to give me a chance, and I'm not ashamed that I've never technically been a producer before, or that I had to take money from her to make it happen. Everyone has to start somewhere and this is where I'm starting." She paused, staring down at him with an uneasy expression. "You can't change your mind. You've already agreed. We have a verbal contract."

"I should have said no," he murmured.

She frowned. "But you didn't," she insisted.

Was he really ready to admit the truth? He'd said yes because she was pretty and funny and she made him feel better about himself. She smelled good and her hair felt like silk between his fingers and he couldn't stop thinking about kissing her. Those were just a few of the reasons that he said yes.

"You asked me for the truth," Marlie said. "And now you need to tell the truth. Why did you say yes?"

"I was intrigued by your ideas. They're good. And it's about time I get back to work."

"It wasn't because I kissed you?"

"Well…maybe a little bit."

"That can't happen again. We have to keep things strictly professional from here on out."

"Of course," Dex said. "I completely agree. And I can do that." He grabbed her hand and pulled her back down next to him.

They stared at each other for a long moment. "You're thinking about kissing me again, aren't you?" She sighed softly. "This is going to be a problem. Maybe we just ought to do it again and get it out of the way so we can move on."

Dex nodded. "You're right, it probably would help."

She drew a deep breath and forced a smile. "So I guess you should just do it and get it over with."

"Right," Dex murmured.

Hell, he knew if he kissed her again, the attraction would never go away. It would just get worse. And then having to pretend that it didn't exist while they worked together would be pure torture. But he wasn't about to refuse her invitation. He wasn't a bloody eedjit.

Dex slipped his hand around her nape, his fingers tangling in her hair. He gently drew her close and touched his lips to hers. But the moment they made contact, he knew he was lost. A need so fierce, so overwhelming, surged up inside him. He wanted to touch her, to kiss her, to tear her clothes off and make love to her until his body was exhausted and his mind was quiet.

Dex took a chance and pulled her even closer, his tongue teasing at her lips, searching for the warmth of her mouth and her unspoken surrender. When she opened beneath the assault, he groaned softly and drew her body on top of his, lying back on the sofa.

He needed this, a chance to clear his head of all

the dark memories, all the twisted guilt that plagued his every waking minute. If he could just find some peace, if only for one night, maybe he could put his life back on track.

As their kiss grew more intense, Dex rolled her beneath him, desperate to feel her body beneath his. He stared down at her, his fingers brushing strands of hair from her face. Her lashes fluttered and the color was high in her cheeks. God, she was so beautiful, so perfect. The prospect of losing himself in her warmth was too tempting to deny.

She opened her eyes, their gazes meeting, and for a moment, he thought she was going to speak.

"What?" he murmured.

"I—I think that's enough," Marlie murmured.

"No," he whispered. "It's not nearly enough." He pulled her into another kiss. But this time, he felt a slight resistance, a hesitation that told him to stop.

Dex drew back and looked down into her flushed face. What the hell was he doing here? He pushed up, bracing his hands on either side of her. "No," he said in a strangled tone.

"No?" A worried look crossed her face. "No to the kiss? Or no to everything else?"

He scrambled to his feet, then raked his fingers through his hair. "No, you're right, we can't do this." He glanced around the cottage. "Bloody hell, what was I thinking? I have to get out of here. It's not you. Really, it's just... I can't make a mess of this."

Dex slowly backed away from the sofa. It took every

ounce of willpower he possessed to grab his jacket, slip on his shoes and walk out the door.

When he reached his truck, he got inside and sat in the dark, listening to the rain pelt the windscreen.

He was in no shape to jump into a sexual relationship, especially one with a woman he was supposed to work with. Sleeping with Marlie would just become another way to quiet his mind when the whiskey and the beer no longer worked.

She didn't deserve that. No woman did. Since Matt's death, he'd been on a dark path, a place that only he could travel. For now, he'd have to be more careful about his selfish needs. He'd focus on the work and let that heal him.

MARLIE OPENED HER eyes to a shaft of sunlight that shone through the bedroom window. The scent of coffee teased at her nose and she sat up, brushing her tangled hair out of her eyes.

She bumped her eye with her wrist and winced at the pain it caused. Touching the spot, she found it tender and swollen. Marlie crawled out of bed and walked out into the living room, the rugby jersey coming down to her knees. Dex was bent over the hearth, building a fire with clods of peat.

"Is there coffee?" she asked.

"In the kitchen," he replied, straightening. He turned to meet her gaze and Marlie saw his expression freeze. "Bloody hell."

"What?"

In three long strides, he crossed the room and

cupped her face in his hands. "I did that. Jaysus, Marlie, I'm sorry."

"What's wrong?"

"You've got yourself a shiner," he murmured. His eyes dropped to her mouth, and Marlie watched the emotion play in his eyes. He wanted to kiss her again, but he was holding back.

Wanting to take away his guilt, she pushed up on her toes and softly touched her lips to his. "Good morning."

"You're not going to think it's so grand once you look in the mirror."

"Oh, I'm sure it's not as bad as you're making it out to be."

"Your eye is purple."

"You'll have to find a way to make it up to me," she said. "You could start by getting me coffee. Very hot, very black."

"I can do that," he said, turning for the kitchen.

Marlie walked over to the fireplace and stood in front of it, staring at her reflection in the mirror hanging above the mantel. The bruise covered the skin beneath her eyebrow and extended to the corner of her eye. The cut was barely visible, but there was noticeable swelling beneath her brow bone.

Dex's reflection appeared in the mirror and she faced him. "It's not that bad," Marlie said, taking the coffee mug from his hands. "Worth it to get you to agree to do my project."

"Our project," he said.

She took a sip of the coffee, regarding him over the rim of the mug. The brew was warm and strong and brushed away the last traces of sleep from her head. "I suppose you're going to demand creative control?"

"Come on, Marlie. I've been making films for years. This is your first. You came to me because you knew I could make something of this project. Now you're telling me that you're not going to listen to me?"

"No. I think it should be an equal partnership. Any differences of opinion will be discussed and we'll come to mutual decisions."

"Someone has to be the boss," he murmured, smoothing his hand over her cheek.

The night had done nothing to quell the attraction between them. Marlie knew it would probably interfere with their working relationship, but perhaps they could pretend that it didn't matter. She could ignore the flood of desire that raced through her body whenever he touched her. She could push aside her own fantasies of what a night with Dex might be and concentrate on the work.

Her professional life was finally coming together. She had the perfect partner to make the documentary with. After it was done, she'd be respected at Back Bay—and maybe even in her overachieving family. She couldn't fail. If she did, all the trust that her grandmother had in her would be destroyed.

"We can't do this," she said. "We can't keep touching and kissing each other. This project is important to me. Really important."

He watched her from across the rim of his coffee cup. "I completely agree," he said. "Not that it's going to be a simple task, but if that's what you want, then I'm all for it. Full stop. No more kissing."

"It's not what I want," Marlie said. "It's what I need."

Dex smiled. "And I'm a bloke who's all about a woman's needs."

Marlie tried to read the meaning in his words, but she couldn't tell if he was serious or just teasing. Everything about him was meant to tempt her, and she wasn't even the kind of woman who was easily tempted.

There had been other men in her life, but her relationships had always fizzled because she wasn't being true to herself or to them. Her professional goals were more important than her personal ones. She didn't want a marriage; she didn't need a family. She'd find all that later, once she'd proved to the world—and to her family—that she had something important to offer.

But then, it was easy to forget about those goals when staring into Dex's handsome face. He'd make any woman question her future plans; Marlie was sure a night in bed with Dex Kennedy would be a life-altering experience. The man was too sexy for his own good.

"I suppose we ought to get some breakfast," he suggested.

Marlie nodded. "I am hungry." She stepped away from him and was headed toward the bedroom when a sound at the door stopped her escape. She glanced over at Dex as she heard a key in the lock. "Should I answer it?"

"No," Dex said.

A few moments later, the intruder pounded on the

door. "Dex? Let me in. You've bolted the door. I'm getting wet out here."

Dex quickly crossed the room and pulled the door open, while Marlie fought the urge to run and hide. Was this some girlfriend of his? Her research had indicated Dex wasn't married, but that didn't mean he wasn't involved.

It was clear from his expression that he knew the woman on the other side of the door. She stepped inside, shaking the rain out of her short dark hair. "It's bucketing out there," she cried. "The road is solid mud, and now I've ruined my new shoes. I tried calling but you left your mobile at my flat." As she pulled the phone out of her jacket pocket, she caught sight of Marlie, dressed in a rugby jersey and nothing else. Her face registered surprise. "Well, hello there."

"Claire, this is Marlie Jenner. She's—"

"Oh, yes," Claire said, moving to Marlie and holding out her hand. "We spoke on the phone. I'm Dex's sister, Claire. What happened to your eye?"

Marlie felt a rush of relief. Dex's sister. Well, at least she wasn't standing in the midst of a completely awkward situation. "Hello. Yes, I recognize your voice now. A door. I ran into a door. Clumsy me."

Claire studied her for a long moment, then shrugged. "I see you've found him. Brilliant. I hope he wasn't too upset with me for revealing his super-secret location. Which, by the way, we will not be letting out for the winter term. The exchange teacher found a flat closer to school." She smiled at Dex. "He doesn't look angry, but with Dex it's sometimes hard to tell."

Dex sighed, shaking his head. "Are you here to make a pest of yourself, or was there a particular reason for your visit?"

"I've just come to pick up some of Nana's belongings. Now that there's no hurry to clean the place up, I thought I'd take them home and go through them there." She glanced from Dex to Marlie. "So will you have any work for me on this film?"

"Are you a filmmaker, too?" Marlie asked.

"No," Claire said. "Just a history teacher. Dex sometimes hires me do research. It helps pay the bills. Especially when I have a brother who doesn't care to work."

"Oh, I'm sure we'll have something for you to do," Marlie said.

"You don't think I could get an introduction to Aileen Quinn, do you? She's my favorite author and I—"

"Enough," Dex said. "Why don't you go get what you came for and be off? We're headed out for breakfast and then we have a full day of work ahead of us. I've got to drive to Dublin and pick up my equipment, and I'm sure Marlie has a list of tasks to tick off."

"I haven't had my breakfast yet," Claire said.

"You're welcome to join us," Marlie offered. In truth, having Dex's sister with them might provide a buffer, a way to avoid the inevitable fantasies about falling into bed with him. She couldn't seem to look at the man without speculating about the body beneath the clothes, and left to her own devices, she might just surrender to temptation and rip every last thread from his body.

"I'm sure you have some papers to grade," Dex said.

"And I'll get back to you on the research. We haven't had a chance to talk much about the film yet."

"Really? Whatever have you two been doing with your time?" She sent her brother a knowing look.

Dex glared at her and Claire decided to beat a retreat. "I'll just go get what I came for."

When they were alone again, Dex smiled apologetically. "Sorry. She can be quite bold, often to the point of annoyance. She thinks because she's my twin sister she has the right to run my life."

"She's your twin?" Marlie envied him. None of her siblings cared much about her. "She's very nice. And I'm sure we can use her on the film. Ian can't do all the research himself. By the way, I'm giving him producer's credit on the film, too."

Dex seemed taken aback by her revelation. "And when were you planning on telling me about this?"

"When it came up in conversation. I wasn't trying to hide it. Besides, he has all the research and it was part of the deal to get Aileen to participate. We need him." Marlie bit her bottom lip. Had she made a mistake? Was Dex going to back out of their agreement now? "I'm sorry. I suppose I could—"

"No," Dex said. "It's not a problem. And you're right. We'll need him."

Marlie drew a deep breath and decided to let the other shoe drop. "I've also given him and Aileen final approval on the film."

Dex gasped. "What?"

"I think you heard what I said. They have final approval."

"Oh, Jaysus, I suppose I should have expected this. Why don't we just hand him the feckin' camera and let him do it outright? A documentary requires a certain distance between the filmmaker and the subject. This can't be some kind of vanity piece. I won't attach my name to something like that."

"It was the deal I had to make."

"No, you didn't have to make any kind of deal. You could have negotiated." He paused, his expression focused. "Did you put this down on paper? Is anything signed?"

"Not yet," she said. "But it'll be fine. Aileen trusts my judgment, and you should, too."

Dex raked his hands through his hair, then cursed softly just as Claire walked back in from the bedroom. She carried a battered suitcase in her arms. "How about some breakfast?" she said in a cheery voice. "Dooly's makes a good fry. They make their own sausage."

The room went silent and Marlie held her breath, praying that everything she'd worked so hard for wasn't about to dissolve before her eyes. "I'm not hungry," Marlie said. "But you two go ahead."

She turned and hurried back into the bedroom, tears of frustration threatening. Slamming the door behind her, she leaned back against it and drew a few deep breaths to calm her emotions. She wasn't going to cry. It would only prove to him what he already believed— that she wasn't prepared to handle a project like this.

She'd bought her way into this job. If it weren't for her grandmother's substantial investment, then she'd still be a production assistant, fetching coffee and photocopying schedules. For all she knew, her grand-mother had funded the entire project, convincing her bosses to give her a shot with a generous donation of cash.

She was a fraud, a pretender, someone who had to rely on nepotism to get ahead. Maybe her family had been right all along. Maybe she didn't have any talent at all. "Don't," she muttered to herself. "If you start to believe it, then it's true."

Why did it make a difference what her family thought of her? She was twenty-six years old and she was still trying to prove herself. A grown woman didn't need to do that. Marlie drew a ragged breath. There were times when she still felt like a child, begging for whatever emotional scraps her parents and siblings were willing to toss her.

She wouldn't be that way with Dex. Provided he even wanted to work with her.

She walked to the bed and threw herself onto it, burying her face in the down pillow. When Dex rapped on the door, Marlie groaned. She'd already made a fool of herself today. If he planned to back out of the film, then she'd rather just move on to her next choice and not discuss it.

The door creaked, but she refused to look up. A few seconds later, she felt the mattress sag. She turned to find him sitting at the end of the bed.

"I'm sorry. I shouldn't have barked at you like that. There was no excuse."

Marlie brushed her hair out of her eyes, watching the regret play across his handsome features. He seemed almost tortured by his behavior. She crawled across the bed and knelt beside him. "I made a mistake. You were—"

"No, I wasn't. This is your project. You're the boss. You make the decisions and you give the orders. I'll do whatever you want."

"But I want us to be partners." She reached out and took his hand, slipping her fingers between his. It felt good to touch him again. "Equal partners. I'll try to talk them out of final approval."

"That would probably be a good idea," he said. "But we'll wait until after we've started filming."

He met her gaze and held it for a long moment. Marlie had to remind herself to breathe. If he'd just kiss her, she wouldn't offer any resistance. She'd pull him onto the bed and let him make love to her for the rest of the day.

But in the end, he just smiled and got to his feet. "Get dressed. It's a long drive to Dublin. We'll grab breakfast along the way."

"You want me to come with you?"

Dex nodded. "Yeah. We'll have plenty of time to talk about the project…boss."

She couldn't help but smile. Everything would be all right. "I'll just get dressed."

"Can I watch?" he teased.

Marlie grabbed the pillow from the bed and threw it at him. "No. There'll be none of that. Now go fetch me more coffee."

He walked out of the room and she flopped back on the bed. Everything was going to be just fine, just fine.

THE RAIN HAD finally cleared, making the drive to Dublin much more enjoyable. Dex was glad to get out of the cottage and leave temptation behind. Alone, with Marlie, he had a hard time focusing on anything but the attraction between them.

Ignoring the desire for the next few months would be difficult, but not impossible. He'd lived in crude conditions, existed on meager rations, stayed up for days straight. He was known in his profession as a guy who could exist in the toughest of conditions. This would just be another test of his willpower.

As they drove northeast through the heart of the Irish countryside, he pointed out landmarks and interesting features while she read portions of the manuscript that Ian Stephens had given her. Their conversation bounced from one subject to another, and Dex was impressed at how knowledgeable Marlie was about documentary filmmaking. Though she may not have served as a producer before, she was aware of a producer's duties and had already put herself firmly in that role for this project.

"We'll need to get decent prints of those photos. Digital copies would be best," he said, pointing to the file that sat on her lap.

"I already have digital copies," she said. "There are some photos of the orphanage that we still have to get from the university archives in Cork. I haven't had much luck there."

"Claire can take care of that," he said. "I'll give you her email and you can contact her directly. I agree with you that we should start by interviewing Miss Quinn.

But we should have at least three or four sessions with her, not just one."

"She's ninety-seven years old—" She cleared her throat. "I'll make arrangements."

"And you're going to interview her. You'll be the on-camera voice. I think you should narrate the film, too. It would be better having a female narrator."

"But I—"

"No," Dex said. "That's the way I see this film. And hear it. It'll be good, you'll see."

An uneasy silence descended on them both as they drove through the outskirts of Dublin. Dex drove directly to the studio that he and Mark had shared, a small loft space in an old pottery in the Stoneybatter neighborhood. He pulled the car into a spot near the entrance and turned off the ignition.

Marlie peered out the window at the old brick building. "Is this it? It's very charming."

Closing his eyes, Dex took a deep a breath, gathering his resolve. He hadn't been back inside the studio since Matt's death. He'd shipped their equipment here from Colombia and called one of their production assistants to unpack everything. Eight months, almost a year, and it still made his gut churn to think of what had happened.

"Are you all right?" Marlie asked.

Dex nodded, opening his eyes. "Yeah. I just need a moment."

"You haven't been back, have you? To your studio."

"No," he murmured.

She placed her hand on his arm, smoothing her

warm fingers over his wrist. "We don't have to do this. We could rent equipment."

Dex chuckled. "Now, that would be silly." He stared down at the spot where she was touching him. His heart slammed in his chest and he wanted to turn and yank her into his arms, to lose his fears in the taste of her mouth and the feel of her body against his. He drew a sharp breath and fixed his gaze at a spot outside. "Let's do it, then."

Dex hopped out of the truck and circled around to open her door. But she'd already jumped out. "I can get my own doors," she said.

"Good to know."

They walked to the entrance, and he unlocked the door and showed her inside. They took the stairs up two flights, but when he opened the door to their space—his space—Dex couldn't bring himself to step inside. He remembered when he and Matt had found the loft, how excited they'd been.

Three years ago. The day he and Matt had realized they'd made it as filmmakers. They'd just returned from Cannes, where their film on Chechen rebels had won an award. They'd spent their prize money on refurbishing the space, bringing in a couple of beds, adding a water closet and shower so they had a place to stay when they were in Dublin.

The loft had been home. A place to drop their equipment between projects, a spot where they met before beginning some new adventure; it was something that he and Matt had built together.

Marlie walked through the door and flipped on the

lights, then turned back to him, holding out her hand. "Show me your studio."

He wrapped her fingers in his and led her through the space, ignoring the ache in his chest and trying to concentrate on the task at hand. He'd just pick up his equipment and leave. He could face the ghosts another day.

Marlie wandered over to the windows and looked down at the street. "You can talk about him," she said softly. "Maybe it would be good to talk about him."

Dex bit back a curse. "I don't think I asked for your opinion on the subject."

"No, you didn't," she said. "But you will tell me. I think you want to."

Dex strode across the room to a wall lined with an industrial rack that he'd filled with his camera equipment. He slowly began to sort through the equipment, then grabbed the aluminum case that held his favorite camera. The moment he picked it up, he froze, the memory of that day coming back to him in full-on Technicolor.

"Jaysus," he murmured, staring at the case. There it was. A bloody handprint on the side. Was it his blood or Matt's? There'd been so much blood everywhere.

"It was my fault," Dex said. "My fault."

He heaved the case across the room and it hit the brick wall with a crash, sending splinters of stone onto the plank floor.

Startled, Marlie looked at him, her eyes wide. Then she calmly walked over to the case and picked it up.

When she saw the bloodstain, she glanced up at him. "I'll just clean this off."

"No, leave it. It's a good reminder."

"Of what?"

"Of my mistakes." He picked up a different camera, then began to gather the rest of the equipment he'd want. "Leave that one. I have another."

"Stop," she said. "Just stop."

"We need to get back on the road," he said. "We've got a long drive."

"We'll stay here for the night," Marlie said. "I've never been to Dublin and I'd like to see some of the city before we leave. We'll drive back tomorrow morning." She forced a smile. "I'm the boss, or so you said."

She looked so beautiful standing there, her chin tipped up, ready for a confrontation. Hell, the last thing he wanted to do was fight with her. Dex wanted to kiss her, and he wasn't about to deny himself the pleasure. Not now.

He slowly crossed the room and then took the case from her hand, setting it at her feet. Drawing a deep breath, he wrapped his arm around her waist and pulled her body against him.

"I—I thought we weren't going to do this," she said in a weak voice.

"I've spent eight months feeling like hell," he said. "And the only relief I get from that feeling is when I kiss you. Are you going to help a poor bloke out, then?"

"You know we're not going to stop at just one kiss."

"I can stop," Dex assured her.

"Maybe I don't want you to," she replied.

He wasn't going to wait for a more explicit invitation. Dex spanned her waist with his hands and drew her into a long, deep kiss. The taste of her was like a narcotic, bringing him an instant sense of relief. She had become his drug of choice.

They stumbled back to his bed, tugging at each other's clothes until they'd both exposed enough skin to explore. Dex pulled her onto the soft down-filled duvet, his lips never leaving hers.

A tiny moan slipped from her throat and he took the opportunity to pull away and look into her flushed face. What were the odds that the fates would gift him with such a perfect woman at the very moment that he needed her most?

He brushed aside the collar of her shirt and pressed his lips to her throat. Her breath came in quick, shallow gasps, and as he moved lower, Marlie tangled her fingers in his hair.

Dex couldn't remember the last time he'd been this desperate. He had to be close to her, to make some kind of connection. But every ounce of common sense told him to take things slow. It didn't have to happen tonight. They had time to savor this attraction and make it last.

With trembling fingers, Marlie reached down and unbuttoned her blouse, brushing the fabric aside to reveal a sexy bra trimmed in lace. Dex pushed up on his elbow and stared down at her breasts. He ran his palm over the soft flesh beneath the satin fabric and her breath caught in her throat.

His body, so tense earlier, suddenly relaxed, as if a tightly wound spring had finally snapped.

Dex curled up beside her, his hand still on her breast, and closed his eyes. This was perfect, he thought to himself. He was safe here, in this bed, with Marlie. He could finally relax.

He drew in a deep breath, the scent of her hair filling his head as exhaustion overwhelmed him. And for the first time in more than a year, he didn't dream.

4

MARLIE STARED AT Dex, watching him sleep. The sun was just brightening the windows of his loft, casting a soft light across his handsome features. She hadn't realized how much tension he carried in his face—or how exhausted he looked. Dark circles smudged the skin beneath his eyes, and he had a permanent wrinkle in his forehead.

And yet, sound asleep, he looked like a completely different man. He seemed almost…boyish, younger and impossibly sexy. Though there was a hard edge to him, she could see how vulnerable he really was. His partner's death had shattered his spirit and he was still struggling to come to grips with it.

It must have been horrible, Marlie mused. She remembered his reaction to the blood on his camera case and she could only wonder what kind of pain he'd felt when he'd been reminded of it all over again.

He'd buried the pain so deep inside of him, but it was like shards of glass, cutting him up from within, working its way to the surface, wounding him at the same time.

There were moments when she felt as if she'd known him forever, times when the connection between them was so strong and real and powerful. She could almost feel him beginning to heal. But then there were other moments when she wasn't sure he would let anybody truly know Dex Kennedy.

Marlie reached out and lightly ran her fingertips over his brow, now void of its usual furrows. At her touch, he stirred and she pulled her hand away, placing it beneath her cheek. Her stomach growled and she winced, closing her eyes.

She'd found some stale cereal in one of the cabinets along with a package of crackers that had provided a late-night snack. But the refrigerator had contained nothing but condiments and bottles of beer. Now she was hungry for something more substantial. Starving, by the sound of her stomach. There ought to be someplace nearby to grab some breakfast before he woke up. She needed a very large cup of coffee and a glazed doughnut or two.

Her stomach growled again and Marlie opened her eyes, only to find Dex awake and staring at her. "Hey," she said, smiling.

"Hey." He frowned. "I fell asleep. Bloody hell, I'm so sorry."

"No, it's fine." She brushed an errant lock of hair from his eyes. "You were tired."

"I must have been completely knackered to fall asleep while seducing you."

"Is that what you were doing?" Marlie teased. "I wasn't quite sure."

Dex looked down at her body. "And we're both still fully dressed. I swear, I'm much better at seduction than I seem. I've never had any complaints, anyway. I've just been a little sleep deprived lately."

"You didn't dream," Marlie said. "At least not bad dreams."

"I didn't give you another black eye?"

"No. See? I survived unscathed."

"Well, there is that," he said. "Well done, Dex."

"You did, however, snore. Just a little bit."

"Oh, now, that must have been very sexy," he said.

Marlie thought she saw a faint blush on his cheeks. Was he really embarrassed or was she just imagining it? Her stomach growled again and Marlie giggled, rubbing her belly with her hand. "Talk about sexy."

"Now, that turns me on," he teased. "Do it again."

Marlie shook her head. "No. I can't."

"You're hungry. We should get you some supper."

"Breakfast. It's morning."

Dex stared at her in disbelief, then pushed up on his elbow, his gaze fixed on the window. "No. The sun's just going down."

"Coming up," Marlie said. "You've been asleep since three yesterday afternoon. It's about eight in the morning, so that's what…seventeen hours?"

"Why didn't you wake me up?"

"I figured you needed the sleep."

Dex sat up and ran his fingers through his messy hair. He shook his head as if to clear his mind and then grinned. "I slept. I mean, I bloody well slept." He drew a deep breath. "I feel good. Do you know how long it's been since I've slept through the night?"

"A long time?"

"Months. I can't remember the last time." He stretched out beside her and wrapped his arm around her waist. "Thank you."

"For what?"

"For letting me sleep. For being here. I don't know. For getting me out of this deep, dark hole I've been living in." Dex grabbed her hand and pulled it to his lips. "I truly do appreciate it. You're an angel."

He gazed into her eyes and a shiver of anticipation skittered down her spine. Was she really ready for this? If he kissed her again, there would be no stopping them. And she wanted to kiss him. She wanted to surrender every last inhibition she possessed and find out what it might be like to have a man as dangerous as Dex Kennedy consume her in his passion.

How easy would it be to get herself wrapped up in an affair with him? He was like no other man she'd ever known—brilliant, talented, worldly, even a little famous. Men like Dex were usually way out of her league. But this seemed so natural, as if they just fit.

Though there still was a need to prove herself to him, Marlie also had something to offer him. Maybe it was just a warm body and a comforting nature, but Dex needed that right now. She could heal him. It was the least she could do for him considering what he was about to do for her.

"Maybe we should get some breakfast," she murmured, twisting her fingers through his.

"Or maybe we should stay in bed," Dex suggested, nuzzling his face into the curve of her neck and pinning her hands above her head.

Marlie drew in a deep breath, closing her eyes and enjoying the feel of his lips on her skin. "Do you really want to do this?"

"Yes," he said. "Absolutely." But then he stopped kissing her and drew back. "But only if you want to."

"I'm not sure. I do. But I don't. And then I do again. Ask me in a minute and my answer will change. Like now, I really do. But afterward, I'm afraid we might realize it was a mistake. And that would be horrible. And really awkward."

"I've never mixed work with pleasure," Dex confessed. "But I have to admit this is the first time I've been tempted."

"Maybe we should hold off and see what develops… organically."

Dex laughed, giving her a dubious look. "Organically? What does that mean? Is that an American thing?"

"It means that I'm tempted, but I want things to develop naturally." A long rumble sounded from the vicinity of her stomach and she groaned. "I'm also really hungry."

"All right. I'll feed you first." He rolled out of bed, then stared down at her. "What the hell am I thinking?" Dex flopped back down on the bed and covered her mouth with his, drawing her into a long, deep kiss.

Marlie moaned softly as she wrapped her arms around his neck. "What the hell?" was right. They were both adults. They could certainly keep sex from interfering with work.

"This is not me seducing you," Dex said. "I just want to make that very clear."

"What are you doing?"

"Just messing around," he said. "Having a bit of a snog."

Giving him a playful slap, Marlie rolled on top of him then straddled his hips. "A bit of a snog? Would that be an organic snog?"

"Mmm-hmm. And I'm about to wear the head off of you."

"That doesn't sound good."

"It means I'm going to kiss you until your lips fall off."

"Oh, that's much better," Marlie said. "Have at it, then, Mr. Kennedy."

He reached up and slipped his hand around her nape, slowly pulling her closer. "It may take me a while, but I think it's a worthwhile goal."

"A black eye *and* no lips?" she murmured. "Just don't mess with my nose. I'm rather fond of my nose."

"I like your nose, too." He cupped her breast in his palm, skimming his thumb over her nipple. "Among some other very lovely body parts of yours, as well."

They spent the next half hour in playful distraction, kissing and teasing and laughing. There was no pressure to tear off their clothes and enjoy each other in more intimate ways, but the need was always there between them, just a kiss or a caress away.

They were dancing on a high wire and it was exhilarating and exciting. She felt beautiful and desired. Marlie knew it would happen eventually. Maybe tonight, maybe tomorrow. They'd have to fall off the wire sometime and indulge their desire. But for now, this was exactly what they both needed.

THEY SPENT THE day exploring Dublin. It was like a mini-holiday, an escape from everyday life, something that was good for both of them.

The more time they spent together, the closer they became—as friends and as business partners. They were learning how to be with each other, how to get along.

Dex showed her all his favorite spots. He took her to see the Book of Kells at Trinity College and the National Museum, soaking in a morning of Irish history. They had lunch at a pub on Grafton Street and then headed to Dublin Castle and walked through the elegant rooms.

Marlie was curious about everything she saw and asked endless questions. He could see her mind working, synthesizing everything they experienced into her plans for the film. And as much as he enjoyed playing tour guide, Dex was looking forward to getting to work.

But his mind wasn't entirely on work. He couldn't help but think about what had happened that morning in his bed. They had stopped denying the attraction between them. It was too obvious to ignore. But neither one of them was quite ready to act upon it.

Dex sensed that when they did, it would be something extraordinary, something beyond just physical pleasure. Though he'd had many different women in his life and his bed, there'd never been one quite like Marlie.

And that frightened him a bit. Here was a girl he could fall for—and hard. She was like a safe harbor in a raging storm, an oasis in the middle of a desert. She was comfort and light, quiet and contentment. And after all the chaos of the past eight months, she made him feel... Happy? Hopeful?

Dex considered the best choice of word. Released. That was it. He felt as though he'd been let out of a prison of his own making, a prison where he'd constantly punished himself for a crime he'd never meant to commit. Now that he was standing in the sunlight again, he was ready to deal with all those dark thoughts and banish them from his mind.

Dex held her hand as they wandered along the Liffey, both of them bundled up against a damp November wind. She stopped to stare at Christ Church Cathedral, her gaze rising to take in the imposing facade.

"Would you like to go inside? Whenever I pass by, I usually go in and light a candle for my grandmother."

"Sure," Marlie said. "When did your grandmother die?"

"Three years ago. Claire and I lived with her when we were younger. She was a grand woman, so kind and encouraging. What about your grandmother? You said she's helping finance the film. Is she a fan of Aileen Quinn, too?"

"My grandmother is a fan of anything that will make me a success," Marlie said with a wry smile.

"What about your parents?"

"I come from a family of very famous doctors. So I'm the black sheep of the family." She laughed. "They call me the dumb one. I didn't get a perfect score on my ACTs."

"What's that?"

"College entrance tests. Everything in my family has to be measured and quantified in some way. It started as test scores, IQs, grade point averages. Now, it's all about titles and salaries and real estate holdings. I don't really compete." She turned to him, forcing a smile. "I wish I had a sister like yours. She seems really nice."

"Yeah, she is. When she isn't being a pain in the arse. My folks were actors and didn't spend much time with us when we were young. We moved from place to place. We even lived in L.A. for a time. But then Claire and I came back to Ireland and finished secondary school here. We lived with my grandmother. She's the one who gave me my first video camera. I found it under the Christmas tree when I was fourteen. We used to come back for the holidays and even though she rarely saw us, she knew the perfect gifts to give. I always thought someday I'd tell her story. She led a very exciting life in her younger days."

"You should do it," Marlie said.

"Maybe I will," he said.

"I called Ian this morning and we have our first interview with Aileen Quinn confirmed for tomorrow."

"Good," Dex said. "I'm ready to get started."

"And I'm getting really nervous," she said.

He slipped his arm around her shoulders as they walked toward the cathedral. "You'll be fine. If you have questions or worries, just ask."

Marlie turned to him. "Have I told you how grateful I am that you agreed to do this?"

"Yes," Dex said, nodding his head. "You have. Many times. I think you can stop thanking me."

"This is a big deal," she said. "This could make my career."

"I remember when Matt and I finally felt like we'd made it, after we won a big award," Dex said. Surprisingly, the recollection didn't cause the usual flood of guilt and pain. "We leased the loft and set up shop. We formed a production company. We bought a new camera and some editing equipment. It seems like ages ago."

"You miss him," Marlie said.

"He was like a brother to me. How do they say it? A brother from another mother?" Dex shook his head. "That's the first time I've been able to talk about him without wanting to throw myself off the nearest cliff." He shrugged. "It feels wrong to be happy."

"It's not," Marlie murmured. She pushed up on her toes and brushed a quick kiss across his lips. "It's good to talk about him."

"We're supposed to be having fun today," he said. "And for that, I think we ought to go have a pint and some supper and then listen to a little music. I'll teach you the Irish way of dancing."

"What is that?"

"Well, first you drink a pint of Guinness. And then you drink another. And then one more. And when you feel like you just don't care about what the world thinks of you, when the place is jammers and the music is crazy, you walk out onto the dance floor and make a holy show of yourself. It's the best sensation in the world."

"I'm game," she said. "When in Ireland, and all that."

"All right. But first I'd like to go in and light a candle. And I should probably ask forgiveness for whatever I might do this evening to embarrass you."

"You're forgiven in advance."

He pulled her to a stop. "Maybe I should stop by the confessional and grab some advance absolution, too?"

"Are you planning on sinning tonight?"

"Yeah, I am," he murmured, pulling her closer. "Hard not to be a sinner when I'm with you."

They walked inside the church, their footsteps echoing on the floor as they slowly strode up the long aisle. They sat in a pew near the front and held hands as they let the silence envelop them. Dex had never been a very religious person, but there was something about sitting in a cathedral like this that reminded him there might be a bigger plan at work than what he was able to discern.

Life had been so good, or so he'd thought. And then Mark had been killed and his world had imploded. And now this beautiful woman had come along and helped him find himself amongst the wreckage. He glanced over at her and smiled.

Marlie caught his gaze and gave him a questioning look. "What?"

"You're really pretty," he said.

"Shh! You're not supposed to say things like that in church."

"You're supposed to tell the truth in church. I'm just saying the truth."

They went back to their thoughts and he said a silent prayer for Matt and his grandmother. But it was difficult to sit beside Marlie and not dream about kissing her. Very improper ideas drifted through his mind and there was nothing he could do to stop them. "Let's get out of here."

He took her hand and they hurried back down the aisle, stopping for a few seconds to light a pair of candles before walking out into the late-afternoon sunshine.

The moment the door closed behind them, he pulled her into his embrace and kissed her, his hands smoothing along the curves of her hips. When he finally took a step back, he noticed an elderly couple watching them from a short distance away. Dex grinned and shrugged, but they just smiled. The old man kissed his wife on the cheek before they continued their stroll.

He'd never dwelled much on finding a woman to spend the rest of his life with. Marriage and family hadn't been part of his plans. His career had been everything to him, and it hadn't been fair to make a commitment to a woman when he spent ten months of the year on the road.

But he wasn't getting any younger. His thirtieth birthday had come and gone, and most of the guys he knew from school were already settled and starting families. Was he really willing to put those possibilities aside? Or would he someday have to make a choice?

Dex pressed his forehead to Marlie's. "It's going to be difficult to get any work done with you around."

"We can spend one more night in Dublin, and then we have to drive back. I feel like I'm not ready. I have to start drafting my interview questions and we need to discuss a script and I—"

Dex kissed her again, effectively silencing her worries. "Then we'd better make tonight count," he said.

"Oh, Danny Boy, oh, Danny Boy, I love you so."

They stood on the sidewalk outside Shaunessy's pub. The sound of a raucous Irish band filtered out into the cool night air and inside, the crowd continued to shout and stomp along to the lively music while Dex serenaded her with his slightly drunken ballad.

It had been a wild night, something that Marlie wasn't accustomed to, but enjoyed because she was with Dex. He'd taught her to dance and they'd played darts and pool and drunk Guinness and eaten chips. It had been a true Irish experience and she had loved every moment of it.

"Dance with me," Dex said, sweeping her into his arms and twirling her around.

She humored him until he reached into his jacket

pocket. Marlie held out her hand. "Give me your keys," she said. "I'm driving."

Dex regarded her in mock astonishment. "You think I'm pissed?"

"If that means drunk, then yes, I think you're just a little bit pissed."

"Can you even drive? Ireland isn't like America. The steering wheel is on the other side, you drive on the other side and it's all very confusing for foreigners and—"

"I know. I've been driving in Ireland for a couple weeks now." She snatched the keys out of his hand and put them in her pocket, but he reached over and plucked them out, playfully holding them in front of her face. Marlie wouldn't be deterred, however, and she took them again and tucked them into the front of her bra. "Now try to get them, boyo," she said.

"Oh, I would love to try," he said, a devilish grin curling his lips.

He reached out for the front of her shirt, but she danced away from him. "Maybe we ought to take a cab," she suggested. "We can come get your truck in the morning."

"I trust you. You can drive. Unless *you're* pissed."

Dex opened the driver's-side door for her and helped her inside, then jogged around to the other side. When he was inside, she pointed to his seat belt and he dutifully fastened it. "Drive on," he said.

"Which way?"

"Down to the corner and then left. And then straight on until I tell you."

Though she'd driven an economy-size rental car on the country highways, she had yet to drive in a large city. The streets were so narrow and Dex's SUV was huge. "I can do this," she murmured as she started the BMW.

She took the first few miles very cautiously, and Dex warned her when she was coming too close to the parked cars along the streets. Thankfully, the traffic thinned when they left the center of the city and got closer to his loft.

Marlie gripped the wheel with white-knuckled hands and kept her eyes fixed on the street in front of her. When she finally pulled up into an empty parking spot, she let out a tightly held breath.

"Well done, you!" Dex said. He jumped out of the car and ran around to her side, but once again, she beat him to the punch. So he took the opportunity to trap her against the door, his hands on either side of her body. "You are an amazing woman, Marlie Jenner. Simply amazing."

He bent close and kissed her, his tongue tracing the crease of her lips. She opened beneath the gentle assault and he pressed into her, their hips meeting. He wasn't quite as drunk as she'd thought he was. In truth, he seemed perfectly capable of seducing her.

"Don't start something you aren't going to finish," she warned, splaying her fingers across his chest.

"Is that a challenge?" he asked. "Because I'd be happy to take that challenge and finish this upstairs. It is too cold out here to be messing around in the nip."

His hand slid down her to waist, then skimmed beneath her sweater, his fingers cool on her bare skin. She closed her eyes as he gently drew her into another kiss, finally allowing herself to feel the desire coursing through her body.

It had taken so much energy to fight it, but with every hour that passed, she found her resolve weakening. She knew it was a bad idea, but she was past caring. He needed her, and she sensed it was about more than just physical release. It was about forgiveness.

He pulled her toward the door, stumbling slightly as he walked backward. They climbed up the first flight, then stopped to enjoy themselves a bit more.

He turned Marlie to face him, his back against the brick wall, the streetlight filtering through the old window beside them on the landing. His fingers worked at the buttons of her blouse, and when it was open, he yanked it off her shoulder and pressed his mouth to her neck. But it wasn't enough for him, and he twisted his fingers in her bra strap and pulled it down until he exposed the pale flesh of her breast.

In the meager light, Marlie watched as he took in the sight of her, smoothing his hands over her breast. He bent forward and pressed a kiss to the spot above her nipple, and Marlie tipped her head back, furrowing her fingers through his hair.

It felt so good, this intense need and the certainty that it would finally be satisfied. He was already hard, and she ached to strip off the clothes that blocked his exploration of her body. Her fingers raked along the taut fabric of his jeans, his erection evident beneath the faded fabric.

Dex dropped a line of kisses to her nipple, then gently sucked it into his mouth, teasing at the tip until it grew hard.

"Are we really going to do this?" she asked, pulling him closer.

He looked up at her and she saw the desire in his eyes. But then a tiny frown marred his expression. He opened his mouth to speak, but snapped it shut and shook his head.

"What?" Marlie asked, turning his gaze back to hers. "No, no, no. Don't stop. It was just a rhetorical question."

"No. You don't want to do this with me," he said, gently pushing her away. "I don't know what the hell I'm doing. What am I doing?"

Marlie felt as if she'd been doused with cold water. His mood had shifted to the opposite extreme. A few minutes ago, he was goofy and playful. And now a cloud had come over him and his expression had turned dark. "Why do you say that?"

"You're too sweet and trusting, Marlie. And I just want to feel normal again. That's no reason to take you to bed, just so I can experience something good again. I'm taking advantage of you."

"You're not." She pulled him close and kissed him, her hand holding tight to his head. "You're just hurt. I can make the pain go away. I want to do that for you."

He sat down on the steps and covered his face with his hands. "I'm drunk."

Marlie wasn't sure what this all meant. Whenever they seemed to get close, he found a way to step back, to throw up a wall between them. She sat down next to him, drawing her shirt closed and tucking her hair behind her ears. "You can't keep punishing yourself like this."

She glanced over to find him staring at her. Marlie drew in a deep breath, knowing that what she was about to say could drive them apart permanently. But it had been clear from the start that his partner's death was still haunting him. "It's not your fault that he died. Bad things happen. Sometimes there's nothing we can do to stop them."

"You don't know that," he said.

"Then tell me," Marlie urged. "It's not going to make a difference in how I feel about you." She spread her palm on his chest. "I know you're a good man, Dex."

"I'm not."

He covered his face with his hands, as if he couldn't bring himself to look at her. Marlie waited, wondering what was so bad that he couldn't say it out loud. "Tell me," she said.

"You're wrong. It was my fault he died." The words seemed to tumble out of his mouth, as if he couldn't stop himself from confessing. "We were ready to leave that morning. We had the plane, and we were all packed up. We were done, but then Matt wanted to go back and get just one more shot. I told him we didn't need it." He paused as if struggling to express himself. "I had a feeling that something was going to happen. But he insisted he needed the shot. And I—I didn't fight him. I should have fought, should have insisted. I sensed it would go wrong and I just ignored my intuition."

"But it was his decision," Marlie said.

"No. If I had just pushed harder, he would have gotten on that plane. I could have refused to go."

The pain in his eyes was almost enough to bring her to tears. He'd been torturing himself all these months with doubts about his decisions, keeping his secrets and letting them fester inside him.

Marlie gently pulled his hands away from his face, weaving her fingers through his. She kissed him, and though he resisted at first, he finally gave in. Dex pulled his hands from hers and cupped her face in his palms, his tongue plunging deep into the warmth of her mouth.

It was as if the kiss was his absolution, forgiveness that he was desperate to possess. Marlie smiled at him through her tears and he shook his head. "I've made a real hames of this, haven't I?"

Marlie giggled, brushing away her tears. "I have no idea what that means." She took his hand and pulled him to his feet. "But I think it's time you took me to bed."

5

DEX OPENED THE door to the loft and followed Marlie inside. He'd been carrying around his guilt about Matt's death for so long, letting it drag him down. And now that he'd finally said it out loud and confessed his complicity in the tragedy, he felt that he could deal with it. It was real and not just a product of his imagination.

Strangely elated, he closed the door behind them and then walked across the room to join Marlie in the small galley kitchen. She opened the fridge and pulled out a bottle of water, then handed it to him. "Do you have any aspirin?" she asked.

"I'm not that drunk," Dex assured her.

"It's for me. I have a bit of a headache."

"Sure," Dex said. He found a bottle in the cabinet above the sink and opened it for her, then handed her his bottle of water. She took two tablets, then followed it with a long drink of water.

He pressed his fingers to her temples and gently

massaged. "I didn't mean to give you a headache," he said.

"It wasn't you. I think it was a mix of the music and the dancing and the beer. I'm not used to partying so hard. I normally spend my nights at home, reading and watching old movies."

"We've got a pretty decent collection of documentaries here," he said. "And the whole Godfather series. We're a little light on the romances, though."

"I'm all right."

He nodded. "Maybe it would help if I kissed you. The best thing for a headache is to get the blood moving, right?" She closed her eyes and he bent close and kissed her left eyelid. Then he moved to her right.

A tiny sigh slipped from her lips and she smiled, her eyes still closed. "Are you going to remember this in the morning?" she asked.

"Look at me," he murmured.

Marlie opened her eyes.

"There isn't one second we've spent together that I don't remember. Tonight isn't going to be any different."

He picked her up and set her on the edge of the counter, then stepped between her legs. There was something about kissing Marlie that he found completely addictive.

Dex wrapped her legs around his waist and carried her to the bed, their mouths still locked in a passionate kiss. When he finally set her down, they began to undress each other, tossing aside each item of clothing until they were both down to bare skin. Breathless, Dex stepped back and looked at her.

He'd imagined this moment a hundred times over the past few days, not always certain it would happen yet hopeful that it would. She reached out and placed her palm on his chest. With a touch as light as a feather, she explored the expanse, her hands outlining every muscle before moving on.

Her fingertip found the scar on his side and she pushed up to examine it more closely. "This is where you were shot?" she asked.

"Through and through," he said. "I have one on the back of my thigh, too."

She pressed a kiss to the healed wound, then stopped. Dex gave her time, knowing that she was considering the ramifications of what they were about to do. He could see it in her expression, in the way she hesitated to take her caress even further.

But then she suddenly got a surge of confidence and she wrapped her fingers around his stiff shaft. His breath caught in his throat as a rush of sensation raced through his body. He hadn't expected to react so intensely, and he fought against the need to immediately surrender.

Her touch was tantalizing, so perfect, as if she already knew exactly how he liked it. Every reaction was more exquisite, more enticing, but he was growing impatient.

Slowly, Dex lowered her onto the mattress, stretching his body out above hers, their hips pressed together.

He braced his hands on either side of her head, bending close to steal another kiss.

They'd left words behind and now communicated through soft sighs and low moans. His fingers found the spot between her legs and he rubbed gently until she began to writhe beneath him. Dex was surprised at how quickly she responded, how close he was able to bring her with just his touch.

But he wanted more than that. He slid down along her body, pressing his mouth to her silken skin, tasting the sweet flesh of her breasts before moving on. When he'd reached his destination, he gently parted her legs and began a tender assault.

Her body trembled and her pleas became desperate, but he continued to tease her toward release. And when he knew she was ready, Dex found a condom in the bedside table and quickly sheathed himself. A moment later, he was there, probing at her entrance.

Marlie grabbed his hips and pulled him against her, bringing her legs up along his thighs. She shifted, arching against him. In the space of a heartbeat, he was inside her, buried deep, her warmth enveloping him.

Dex held his breath, trying to maintain his self-control. But Marlie was already too close, and the moment he moved she dissolved into shudders and deep spasms. It was enough to test his resolve and he drove into her in long, even strokes. She whispered his name and he stared down into her flushed face, watching as she worried at her bottom lip with her teeth.

It had been a long time since he'd been this alive, this aware. Every nerve in his body vibrated with pleasure, and when his release was near, it felt as if an electric current were traveling through his bloodstream. He froze, trying to keep himself from tumbling over the edge. But it was no use. He was already there.

He grabbed her legs and sank down on top of her as his body dissolved in the sweet satisfaction of his orgasm. Marlie's fingers clutched at his shoulders and he jerked again, unable to stop the spasms. It went on longer than he'd ever experienced and when it was over and he was completely sated, Dex collapsed at her side, gasping for breath.

It hadn't gone exactly how he'd planned, but then, neither one of them had been patient enough for a long, slow seduction. That would come later. For now, they'd both preferred a headlong race to the finish.

He turned his head to find her watching him, and Dex smiled. She reached out and ran her thumb along his bottom lip. "I don't think you're drunk anymore," she whispered.

"I never really was," he replied. Dex rolled to his side and slipped his hand around her nape. "You are the most beautiful woman I've ever known."

"You don't have to say that."

A pretty blush stained her cheeks and she looked away, but he returned her gaze to his. "You brought me back. I didn't think I'd ever feel this way again."

Marlie threw her leg over his hip and ran her foot along the length of his leg. "Does that mean you don't want to do it again?" she asked.

"I think I can manage. Just give me a moment to collect myself."

They lay next to each other in the soft light and talked about silly things. Marlie had an uncanny way of reading his mood and finding a way to make him feel as if he didn't have a care in the world. In just one night, he laughed more than he had in the past year.

"Do we really have to make this documentary?"

Marlie gasped. "You don't want to? But I thought—"

"No, I do. I do. But I'd much rather grab a flight to some tropical island and spend the next month doing nothing but this—and getting a decent suntan."

"Maybe we could do that when we're done?"

"That might work," he said.

"Where would we go?"

"I spent a week in the Seychelles. I'd love to take you there. And from there we could go to Cape Verde. Or maybe we could go to Belize."

"I think we should focus on the film first and the fun later," she said.

"You are a proper boss, aren't you?" Dex teased.

"I am."

"Are there any other orders you'd like me to follow, boss? Can I do anything for you—fetch you a drink, fluff your pillows?"

"You know what I'd do if we were in Boston right now? I'd call out for a pizza."

"We do have pizza in Dublin," Dex said. "And Indian food and Thai food and—"

"Indian food? Do they deliver?"

He glanced at his watch. "I don't know. It's pretty late." Dex leaned off the bed and grabbed his jeans, then pulled his mobile out of his pocket. "What do you want? Your wish is my command."

"Surprise me," she said, giggling.

Dex called a restaurant and ordered the food, but when they wouldn't deliver, he decided to go pick it up. Marlie protested, but he kissed her and crawled out of bed. He tugged on his jeans while she watched from the bed.

"You don't have to do this. I'm not that hungry."

"When the boss gives me an order, I have to follow it," he said. "Just don't go anywhere. I'll be right back."

He quickly finished dressing, then gave her a kiss before he hurried out the door. When he got down to the street, he stood in the doorway for a moment and thought about what had just happened. With the other women in his life, he'd never seen a future for them. But with Marlie, he could easily imagine wanting to spend a lifetime with her. She was so completely open and honest. She didn't play silly games and she knew exactly what she wanted.

He strode to his SUV and got inside. He'd only met her a few days ago. Maybe he'd discover some deeply hidden flaw that would change his opinion. Or perhaps he'd stumbled across "the one" without even realizing it.

He turned the key in the ignition and pulled out onto the street. Dex recalled the long conversations he and Matt used to have about life and love, usually while sitting in some exotic location, drinking beer and eating the local cuisine.

Matt had always believed that he'd settle down and

get married some day. Dex had chosen the opposite side of the argument, insisting that their chosen profession would make marriage impossible. They'd debated the question over and over again, never coming to an agreement.

"I guess you were right, buddy," Dex murmured. "I wish you were here so I could tell you."

THEY DROVE BACK to County Kerry early the next day. Dex's SUV was loaded with the equipment they'd need to start taping the documentary, and it took several trips to unload his gear into the cottage. The closer they got to starting production, the more nervous Marlie became.

It had been easy to have confidence when all she was doing was putting together production schedules and organizing research and writing scripts. Tomorrow they'd actually put something on tape. That would be when the real work began.

And she needed it to be good work. If it wasn't, no one would ever want to buy the film. Dex had assured her that he'd make it wonderful and that they'd get plenty of interest from the national television network in Ireland and from a network in England. And she was sure public broadcasting in America would want it. If she could pull it off.

Marlie stared down at the production schedule she was working on. She couldn't let Dex see what a mess she really was. She had to focus on the job and make sure she covered all her bases. But it was becoming increasingly difficult to think about work when he was distracting her with romance.

When she'd decided to surrender to their attraction, Marlie had realized it was a risk. But it had felt like the right thing to do. He'd needed her. No one had ever really needed her. Her family had barely known she existed and she'd never had a lot of close friends. As for men, they were only interested in turning her into their vision of the perfect girlfriend. Strangely, Dex seemed to like her exactly the way she was.

"Hello! Anyone home?"

Marlie turned in her chair as Dex's sister, Claire, walked through the front door of the cottage. "Hi," she said.

"You are here. I didn't see Dex's truck."

"He had to run a few errands," Marlie said.

"That's odd. He told me to stop by. He had some research he wanted me to do in Cork this weekend."

"I'm not sure what he had in mind," Marlie said. "But he'll be back in a bit. Would you like a cup of tea?"

"Sure. But I'll make it. You go back to your work."

Marlie stood up and stretched her arms above her head. "I need a break. I feel like I'm putting together a jigsaw puzzle while wearing a blindfold." At Claire's questioning look, she smiled. "The production schedule."

"Dex never writes it down. He always has the schedule in his head. He just seems to know what comes next."

"You've worked with him a lot?" Marlie asked.

"I was the assistant producer on his first five films," she said. "We were only fourteen, but they were good films. You should ask him to show you the movies sometime. He has them on his laptop."

Claire slipped out of her jacket and wandered into the kitchen, chatting as she put the kettle on the stove. "I talked to him earlier this morning. He sounded happy."

"He did?"

She walked back into the room and sat down across from Marlie. "He did. Thank you. I'm not sure what you did, but he's doing much better. He was in a very dark place for a very long time."

Marlie smiled, dropping her gaze back to her work. "He just needed something new to focus on."

"And what was that? You? Or the work?"

"A little of both, I think." She wasn't sure whether she ought to reveal more. But Claire knew him better than anyone.

"He blames himself for Matt's death," Claire said. "He and Matt were such good friends. It was like losing a brother."

"We've talked about it. It wasn't his fault. He doesn't really believe that yet, but I think he wants to move on. Although that might be easier said than done."

"He still has a lot of important work to do. He and Matt were going to do a documentary on child labor in the garment industry. They had it all lined up before Matt died. Maybe you could do it with him?"

"No," Marlie said. "I'm really not— I just haven't—

This is my first film. I'm not sure I'm really ready to take on something like that."

"You never know until you try," she said.

The sound of Dex's car interrupted their conversation, and a few seconds later the door opened and he walked inside. He tugged off his jacket. "It is getting really cold out there. We ought to find that tropical island right now and spend our days and our nights stark naked—" He noticed Claire. "What are you doing here?"

"I came to pick up the research work you have for me."

"And I just dropped it off at your flat. Isn't that what I—" He chuckled. "You know, you did say that you were going to stop by. Sorry. My mind had been on…other things."

"No problem. It gave me a chance to talk with Marlie." Claire turned away from her brother. "So, Marlie, tell me about this Ian Stephens. Have you met him? Is he as sexy as he sounds on the phone?" She gave Dex a pointed glare. "And don't tell me I can't mix business with pleasure."

"I would never do that," Dex said, his lips curling up into a grin. "Never."

"He is," Marlie said. "He's tall and dark, kind of nebbishy but in a sweet way. And he has the most gorgeous blue eyes. And he wears glasses. Dark rims."

"Single?"

"I think so. He doesn't wear a ring."

"And how do you know that?" Dex asked.

"Women always check," Claire said. "It's just what we do."

"Did you check when you met me?" Dex asked Marlie.

Claire also turned her attention to Marlie and waited for her answer. Marlie laughed. "Of course I did. I just said, it's what girls do."

His brow arched up and he shook his head. "Right."

"I bet you checked for her ring, too," Claire said. "Don't lie. I know you did."

"A ring does not always tell the tale. Some people don't wear wedding rings," Dex said. "Don't you have someone else to bother?"

"I was just going to have a cup of tea," she said. She glanced back and forth between Dex and Marlie, then grudgingly stood. "All right. I'll leave you to do… whatever it is you're going to do. And I hope you're practicing safe sex. Wear a johnny." She grabbed her jacket and headed to the door. "If you need my help when you're taping Aileen Quinn, I can always bunk school for the day."

"Bunk school," Marlie said after Claire had shut the door behind her. "Play hooky?"

He nodded, then bent close and brushed a kiss across her lips. "We probably should find a way to let her meet Aileen Quinn or I'm never going to hear the end of it."

"Let's just get through the first day of interviews and then we can talk about it."

Dex pulled her to her feet and wrapped his arms around her waist. "Don't worry yourself about the in-

FREE Merchandise is 'in the Cards' for you!

Dear Reader,

We're giving away FREE MERCHANDISE!

Seriously, we'd like to reward you for reading this novel by giving you **FREE MERCHANDISE** worth over **$20**. And no purchase is necessary!

You see the Jack of Hearts sticker above? Paste that sticker in the box on the Free Merchandise Voucher inside. Return the Voucher promptly...and we'll send you valuable Free Merchandise!

Thanks again for reading one of our novels—and enjoy your Free Merchandise with our compliments!

Pam Powers

Pam Powers

P.S. Look inside to see what Free Merchandise is **"in the cards"** for you!

W e'd like to send you two free books

to introduce you to the Harlequin® Blaze™ series. These books are worth over $10, but they are yours to keep absolutely FREE! We'll even send you 2 wonderful surprise gifts. You can't lose!

REMEMBER: Your Free Merchandise, consisting of **2 Free Books** and **2 Free Gifts**, is worth over $20.00! No purchase is necessary, so please send for your Free Merchandise today.

Plus TWO FREE GIFTS!

We'll also send you two wonderful FREE GIFTS (worth about $10), in addition to your 2 Free Harlequin Blaze books!

YOUR FREE MERCHANDISE INCLUDES...

2 FREE Harlequin® Blaze™ Books
AND 2 FREE Mystery Gifts

FREE MERCHANDISE VOUCHER

Please send my Free Merchandise, consisting of
2 Free Books and **2 Free Mystery Gifts**.
I understand that I am under no obligation to buy
anything, as explained on the back of this card.

150/350 HDL F5HT

Please Print

FIRST NAME

LAST NAME

ADDRESS

APT.#   CITY

STATE/PROV.   ZIP/POSTAL CODE

NO PURCHASE NECESSARY!

▶ Detach card and mail today. No stamp needed. ▶

© 2013 HARLEQUIN ENTERPRISES LIMITED. ® and ™ are trademarks owned and used by the trademark owner and/or its licensee. Printed in the U.S.A.

H-B-12/13-FM-13

terviews. You'll be fine. You got me to reveal all my secrets. You'll do the same for Aileen Quinn."

"You were drunk," she said.

"Not so. I was feeling no pain, but I was not drunk. Or not *very* drunk."

Marlie slipped her arms around his neck. "I'm glad you told me about Matt. I know it wasn't easy."

"Actually, it was," Dex said. "I don't seem to have any trouble talking to you. Nor do I have any trouble kissing you. Or taking off all your clothes and—"

"I have work to do," she interrupted. "I can't figure out this production schedule."

"We don't need a schedule. Not for this film. We'll just go along, day to day. We really don't have any deadlines. There's no pressure to rush."

"But I want to get it done. The sooner it's done, the sooner we can get it out there and in front of my bosses. And the sooner I can pay back my grandmother."

"We'll get it done," he said.

The teapot on the stove began to whistle and he glanced over his shoulder. "Why don't we turn off the tea and I'll take you out for some lunch. There's a great pub in Killarney that makes the best burgers."

"I have to get this done," Marlie said, pointing to the papers scattered over the table.

He sighed, then scooped up the papers. "We'll take them with us. We can have a working lunch. You can talk, I'll eat."

Marlie groaned. He always seemed to get his way, and yet she was the one who was supposed to make all the decisions. Though she wanted to relax and approach things more the way he did, she just couldn't afford to mess this up. She had too much riding on it. So why was it so hard to say no to Dex?

"All right, all right. Just let me get changed and we can go."

"You look great the way you are."

She reached up to touch the knot of hair on the top of her head. "You've got to be kidding me."

"You do," Dex said. "You always look great to me."

Marlie shook her head. "You'll say just about anything to get me into bed, won't you?"

"I'll say anything to get you to go to lunch. I'm as weak as a salmon in the sandpit."

Marlie walked to the bedroom. "I'm not even going to ask about that one."

"I can help you dress," he said, following after her. "I'm really good with your bra, don't you think?"

Claire was right. He was like a different man now, so funny and sweet, always teasing. The dark cloud that had seemed to hang over him had disappeared, at least for now.

Sleeping together had been the right thing for him… but would it cost Marlie her career?

DEX STOOD BEHIND the camera, watching the monitor as Aileen Quinn spoke, her words soft and lilting. He'd been listening to Marlie interview the author for the past two hours, and with each question she asked, he became more convinced that she had an extraordinary talent. From the moment they'd started talking, Marlie had made her subject feel comfortable and relaxed.

Within minutes, she'd developed a trust with her subject that was hard for many professionals to achieve.

There was a very subtle art to interviewing, and Marlie came by it naturally. Already, Aileen had revealed some interesting incidents in her life, the kind of revelations that would make for a great story. Though he wasn't yet sure he'd have control over the final edit, Dex decided that if Aileen was revealing a story to the camera, it was fair game.

As he studied the elderly woman, he was relieved that Marlie's instincts about the film had been right. Even though this was just the first day of interviews, he could see how it would all fall into place—the interview footage, the archival photos and film, the commentary from her long-lost relatives. It would make a powerful narrative.

Dex stepped away from the camera as Aileen began a story about the first time she'd fallen in love. Her eyes were bright and she spoke directly into the camera as she wove her story. He could imagine her as a young woman, about Marlie's age, trying to find her place in the world after a difficult childhood.

He watched Marlie, her attention completely engaged in the conversation. Every now and then, she'd scribble a few notes. When there was a pause in the conversation, she'd carefully frame a question and it would start Aileen down another interesting path.

When Aileen finally fumbled a response to a question and asked for a retake, Dex realized the older woman was growing tired. He held up his hand and Marlie quickly called a break. Sally appeared instantly at the door with a pot of tea and a plate of freshly baked shortbread biscuits. She offered Dex one, then poured Marlie a cup of tea.

"If you'll excuse me, I'm going to stretch my legs," Aileen said, reaching for her cane. "You two enjoy your tea and I'll be back in about fifteen minutes."

"We can break for the day," Dex said. "I've got cutaways I can film with Marlie."

"No, no," Aileen said. "I can go a bit longer. This really is rather enjoyable. Nice company." She walked out of the room, Sally following close behind her.

"It's going well," Dex said as he raised his arms above his head, working a kink out of his neck. "You were good. Very good."

"Really?" A wide smile broke across her pretty face. "It was good, wasn't it? I mean, I don't know why I was so worried. Once she started talking, the questions just came to me. I didn't even look at my notes."

"It's going to make a great film," Dex said as he switched off the lights.

As he passed the bookcases that lined one wall, Dex perused the framed pictures that he'd noticed from across the room. "Do we have copies of all of these?"

"I'll make sure," Marlie said. "Ian will know."

"What about pictures of her brothers?"

"We got some nice ones from their heirs. And I'm hoping the archives might have a photo of Aileen's father. Since he was killed in the uprising, there might be a photo published somewhere. We have only one of Conal, though. He's the one who still hasn't been found." She pulled a photo from her folder. "We think this is him. He resembles the others."

Dex felt an instant recognition when he examined the old photo. But there was no way he could possibly know the man. The picture was at least sixty, maybe seventy years old, and Conal wore a British soldier's uniform. "Are you sure this is him?"

"Yes. Ian believes so. Conal fought with the Brits during the Second World War, but after that, he just disappeared. There's speculation that he may have deserted, but Ian has had trouble getting confirmation from the British army. If he did desert, he may have taken on a new identity. Aileen hopes that if we show his photo around, someone, somewhere will recognize him."

"Right," Dex murmured. He handed her the photo, but he couldn't rid himself of the odd sensation that he'd seen the photo before. But where would he have—?

A faint memory worked its way to the front of his mind. Dex reached into his pocket and pulled out his mobile, then dialed his sister's number. She was still in class, so he left a message. "Claire, I need that suitcase full of photos you took from Nana's house. Can you drop it by the cottage when you have a chance? I'll ring you later."

Marlie shot him a curious look. "What's going on?"

"Nothing," he said. "Just…something I want to look into. Nothing important." He took her hand. "Come on, let's have a walk in the garden. It's a sunny day and we've got all of ten minutes to find an appropriate bush."

"Why do you need a bush? Aileen has a perfectly good bathroom."

"I need a bush so I can pull you behind it and kiss you," he said.

Marlie shook her head. "No. You're just going to have to wait. Not here."

"Why not here? No one is looking. Just a quick snog and that's it."

"No! We have to maintain a professional relationship while we're working."

He growled playfully, trying to catch her hand as they walked onto the rear terrace. "Then I'll just have to imagine how soft your lips are. And how sweet your mouth tastes. And how smooth your skin is when I—"

Marlie pressed her finger to his lips, then quickly gave him a kiss. "There. Will that hold you?"

Dex laughed. "No. Not even close." He grabbed her and dragged her into a deep, delicious kiss, taking care to make sure it was a kiss she'd be thinking about for the rest of the afternoon. Kissing Marlie had taken on a special excitement for him now that he knew it could be a prelude to activities much more intimate.

An image of the passion they'd shared the night before flashed in his mind, and Dex would ensure they'd enjoy the same thing tonight, and every other night they spent together. There wasn't any reason to deny themselves. And today had proved that they could get along just fine on a professional level, even if they were tearing it up at night in the bedroom.

"All right, that's enough," she said, dancing out of

his embrace. She walked over to the low stone wall, staring out at the formal gardens.

Dex joined her, sitting down on the wall and toying with her hand. "There is one other thing we should talk about. You need to go back and press Aileen about her affair with Geoffrey Willis. You sort of glossed over it and it's an important part of her life. They carried on for nearly six years. He was an influential politician."

"No," Marlie said.

"No?"

"It's just not important. She told us what she wanted us to know."

"Six years of her life wasn't that important? She said she loved him and then he ran off and married a woman half his age. Aren't you curious how that shaped the woman she became? She didn't address the breakup at all. Did she dump him or did he dump her? The viewer will want the details."

"It's too painful for her," Marlie said, moving away from the wall. "Can't you see that?"

"What I see is that it makes *you* uncomfortable because you're too close to your subject. If you can't ask her the hard questions, maybe I should."

"No!" The chilly breeze whipped at her hair and she tucked it behind her ear. "I'm the boss and this is my decision. You agreed that's the way it would work."

"I didn't agree to you chucking cream-puff questions at her," he said. "This is an important point. Maybe one of the most important. It's why she never married, don't you understand that?"

"No, I don't. And I think it's presumptuous of you to

assume that a woman's life is defined by the men she's loved. Maybe Aileen chose not to marry. Or maybe she just never found a man worth loving. There are lots of reasons why a woman might not marry, and I'm not going to push Aileen to reveal something she'd rather keep to herself. That's the end of it." She started for the door, but his words stopped her.

"It's not," he called. "If you don't ask her, I will."

Marlie spun around. "If you do, I'll fire you."

Dex chuckled and walked past her to the door. "No, you won't. Because you know I'm right." He opened the door and stepped back inside. "Are you coming?"

With a low curse, she stalked past him and headed back to the library. Aileen was waiting for them, seated in the wingback chair she'd been in earlier, a cup of tea in her hand. She frowned as she took in Marlie's expression, and Marlie forced a smile. "Just a little creative disagreement," she said.

Aileen's eyebrow arched and she looked at Dex. "Oh, I see."

"Are we ready, then?" Dex asked. "Or would you like another cup of tea?"

"I'm ready," Aileen said. "Where do you want me to start?"

"Actually," Dex said, "I'd like you to go back and talk a little bit more about your relationship with Geoffrey Willis."

Marlie shot him a murderous glare and mouthed the word "no." But Aileen merely nodded.

"Of course," she said. "We did gloss over that period in my life, didn't we?"

Marlie stiffened as the elderly woman repeated Dex's words. Had she overheard their argument on the terrace?

Marlie cleared her throat. "Miss Quinn, if you'd rather not talk about it, you don't have to."

"My dear, I'm ninety-seven years old. I've lived a long and very satisfying life. And if I don't tell all my secrets to you, just who would I tell them to?"

"I think that's a brilliant attitude to have, Miss Quinn," Dex said, reaching over to switch on the lights.

"And I think you're used to getting exactly what you want, Mr. Kennedy. You wield your charm well."

Marlie sat down in her spot and opened her notebook. "All right, let's continue." She waited for Dex to turn on the camera, and when he pointed to her, she continued. "Miss Quinn, let's talk more about Geoffrey Willis. You said you met through mutual friends. Can you describe your meeting?"

Dex smiled to himself. Yes, she could be stubborn. But at least she was willing to learn from her mistakes. As a filmmaker, she should never leave any stone unturned. She couldn't fear the truth. But as he watched Aileen in the monitor, his mind drifted back to her argument.

Would she one day consider their affair just a mistake she'd made? And when she was an old woman, how would she remember him? Would it be with anger or fond feelings? Or would she forget him entirely?

6

THEY LEFT AILEEN'S just before 4:00 p.m. The author had invited them to stay for dinner and Marlie wanted to accept, but Dex insisted that they had a lot to talk about before returning the next day.

Marlie suspected that their discussions would have nothing at all to do with tomorrow's filming schedule, and everything to do with the argument they'd had on the terrace.

As they sped toward the cottage, Marlie kept her thoughts to herself. She wasn't willing to admit that once again, he'd been right. Once she'd pressed, Aileen had offered so much more detail about her love affair with Geoffrey Willis, and they never would have gotten the footage if Dex hadn't asked the first question.

"Are you ever going to talk to me again?"

She glanced over at him. "Of course. It would be pretty hard to work together if we didn't speak. I just don't feel like talking to you *now*."

"I did what I thought was best for the film," Dex

said, staring out the windshield, his hands gripping the steering wheel. "You hired me because I'm good, and now you don't want me to be good. How does that make feckin' sense?"

"Don't curse at me," Marlie said.

"I didn't curse."

"You don't think I know what *feckin'* means?"

"Why are we arguing? I did my job, Marlie, and if you have a problem with that, then maybe you *should* fire me."

Another long silence spun out around them both, the only sound the slap of the wipers on the windshield. She'd tried to let it go, but his intransigence had been such a surprise. "Remember how you said I'd be the boss? Was that just lip service or did you mean what you said? Because I don't understand how you could ignore my wishes if you were taking all your orders from me."

Cursing, Dex jerked the steering wheel sharply and the SUV veered off the road onto a rutted lane. They were driving toward the water, bouncing around with every bump they crossed. Marlie held tight to the hand-grip above the door. She braced her other hand on the ceiling of the passenger compartment.

"Answer this. Was the footage we got good?"

"Yes."

"Is it something we can use?"

"Yes."

"All right. Can we stop arguing now?" Dex asked. "It's done. There's no use going over it again."

But Marlie wasn't ready to let go. What was the use

of ground rules if he was just going to ignore them? "We had an agreement."

"Well, that agreement isn't working for me. Marlie, you have to let me do my job and trust that I'll do it well. If you don't trust me, then we're going to have a helluva time trying to get along."

"I do trust you," she snapped, frustration coloring her tone. In truth, she'd never trusted a man as much as she trusted Dex.

He pulled the truck to a stop at the edge of a cliff overlooking the water. The sea was gray and angry, whitecaps driven across the surface by the wind. "What are we doing here?"

"Wait here," he said.

Marlie watched as he jumped out of the truck. He left the wipers running, the blades clearing the raindrops off the front window. Dex walked to the edge of the cliff. He balled up his fists and tipped his head back, and from what she could discern, he was shouting something into the wind.

She opened the door and jumped out, then trudged through the mud toward him. "What are you doing?" she screamed.

He spun around and faced her. "Nothing!"

"You're doing something. Why are you yelling at the ocean?"

"Because I don't want to yell at you," he said.

"Why not?"

"Because I don't want to fight with you. We get along so well, and I don't want to ruin everything between us just because you're driving me stark raving mad."

"You won't ruin anything. Just tell me how you feel."

He stared at her for a long moment. "This is a trick, isn't it? You really don't want to know how I feel. If I tell you, you're only going to get more angry at me."

"I won't," she said. "Just say it."

"All right. You're being a giant pain in the arse. I'm trying to do my job but I'm afraid to because it might offend you or upset you. I know what I'm doing, and I know what this film should be. So I'd appreciate it if you'd just trust me."

"I thought we were partners."

"And I thought you were the boss. And as the boss, you should want what's best for this project. See my problem here? The rules keep changing. Do you want absolute control or do you want a great film? Your choice."

Raindrops ran down her cheeks and clung to her lashes. She brushed them away. He was right. He should be in charge. She was stupid to believe that she was experienced enough to call all the shots. "All right," she said. "You should be the boss, then."

She strode back to the truck and got inside. He followed a few moments later and when he crawled in beside her, they sat in stony silence, listening to the rain on the roof. Marlie felt the frustration welling up inside her, but she refused to let herself give in to the emotion. It was a practical decision, and now that she'd made it, she knew it was right.

They'd been shooting just one day and already she'd made a complete mess of everything. Her coproducer didn't trust her, she'd insulted his professional skills, they were in the midst of a power struggle and she was dripping wet. "Just take me home."

"That's another thing," he said. "If you're planning to stay at the cottage, why is all your stuff still in a hotel room in Killarney?"

"In case I need to get away from you," she murmured.

Dex sighed. "I don't want you to get away from me," he said. He turned and draped his arm across the back of the seat, his fingers toying with her hair. "See? This is good. We're discussing our differences."

"We're fighting," she said stubbornly.

"This isn't fighting," he said. He gently drew her closer.

Marlie's anger slowly dissolved. She needed to learn to let go, to be more collaborative and not try to control every single detail.

"Maybe we should kiss and make up?" Dex asked.

"I don't want to make up," Marlie said.

"Yes, you do. You want to kiss me."

She shook her head. "Nope."

"I'll just give it a little try. You'll be convinced. It'll be nice."

He touched his lips to hers and in that moment, Marlie realized that being angry with him was a waste of time. She was falling in love with Dex, and even when he was acting like an ass, she still couldn't help herself. With a soft groan, she slid across the seat and climbed onto his lap.

He helped her out of her jacket and then pulled her sweater over her head. The windows of the truck were already beginning to fog over, and her breath, coming in gasps, clouded between their faces.

She lost herself in a deep kiss, her tongue teasing at his. Though the air was cold, his hands were warm, and she arched into his touch.

As darkness surrounded the truck, Marlie felt as if they were entirely alone in the world. The wind-driven rain pelted the truck, drowning out the sound of her heartbeat. Slowly, they struggled out of their clothes, removing just those that were in the way and pushing the rest aside.

When she finally freed him from his jeans, Marlie had all but forgotten their fight. It didn't make any difference what happened during the workday. This was all that really mattered, this desire burning between them. As long as they had passion, they'd weather any disagreements.

"This car was not made for seduction," he said, tugging at her skirt. "We could hurt ourselves."

"That might be fun," Marlie said, sending him a wicked smile. She loved the experience of being completely out of control. It was so exhilarating. "Please tell me you brought a condom."

Dex twisted around to pull his wallet from his back pocket and produced a small package. "I put two in my wallet this morning."

"Two? You thought we were going to use two in a day?"

"A bloke can hope, can't he?" Dex asked.

They continued to tease each other, and when she finally smoothed the condom over his hard shaft, all she could think about was the wonderful sensation of him moving inside of her.

Marlie slowly lowered herself, taking him in, inch by inch, until he was buried deep inside her. Their gazes locked and never wavered as she rose and then sank back down again.

At first she moved slowly and deliberately, but then he reached between them and began a tantalizing caress. Marlie's focus wavered, and she closed her eyes and concentrated on his touch and the sensations that raced through her body.

He kept her close for so long, playing her body with a skill she could barely comprehend. He knew when she was teetering on the edge and pulled her back from it, then started again. Marlie was sure her release would be powerful. Her body trembled, and then, without warning, the first spasm stuck.

"Yes," he murmured as she cried out in surprise. "That's what I wanted."

Marlie collapsed against him, her body surrendering to the exquisite wave of pleasure. Dex followed her a few moments later, giving in to his own desires. And when they both were completely spent, he kissed her, his lips soft against hers.

"I guess that was make-up sex?"

"Mmm," Marlie said.

"It was sort of amazing. Why is that?"

"I don't know. Maybe because we were close to being over just fifteen minutes before?"

"Can we have make-up sex all the time?"

Marlie pulled back and smiled. She ran her fingers through his rain-dampened hair. "Well, we're probably going to fight again. I can't see us getting through this film without a few more disagreements."

"Good," he murmured. "I'm looking forward to our next fight. Can we have one tomorrow?"

She giggled. How would she ever be able to argue with him again, knowing that all he was thinking about was make-up sex? "We're not going to fight anymore. We're going to have constructive discussions about our differing opinions."

"You take the fun out of everything," he said.

"I do not!" Marlie cried. She reached out and pinched his chest. "Take it back."

"Oh, don't be such a puss face and give me another kiss."

Would there ever be a disagreement so bad that they couldn't solve it with great sex? Even as she pondered the question, she knew that their relationship was based on much more than physical attraction. She just wasn't sure what that meant.

"WHY ARE WE taking a day off," Marlie said to him, "and driving all the way to Cork? We're a full week into production and I really should be working on the script. And Claire said she had some questions about the research she's doing."

"This is important," Dex said. "There's something you need to see."

"Can we at least stop by the archives?"

"We can," he said. "If we have time."

Dex turned right onto Sunday's Well Road and they drove along the river. She wasn't going to like what he was about to show her, but it was important that Marlie see it. She had to understand what documentary filmmaking was about, and that as a producer, she must face the difficult choices.

Dex turned right again on Convent Avenue and a minute later, the crumbling facade of the Good Shepherd Convent came into view. He'd made arrangements to scout the site and had a key to get inside both the gate and the main building. Still, from what he'd heard, a key wasn't necessary. Most nights, the local gougers used it as a place to drink and get high. It was usually safe to explore during the daylight hours, though.

He pulled the SUV to a stop near the iron gate, posted with signs warning off any intruders.

"What is this?" Marlie asked.

"It's the old Good Shepherd Convent and the site of one of Ireland's Magdalene laundries." He opened his door and stepped out, and Marlie quickly followed him. Dex had read all the stories about the cruelty and abuse suffered by the women who'd been locked away at the convent. He and Matt had even discussed making a film about it. They had come here five years ago to look at the place, but then another project had captured their interest and they left this one for another time.

"Why did you bring me here?" she asked as he unlocked the gate.

"It's important for you to see this." They walked down a narrow, brush-lined path, so overgrown that it was barely wide enough for them to walk side by side. When they stepped into the light, the imposing redbrick buildings stood against the blue sky.

"Come on, let's go in."

"It's locked up," Marlie said.

"I have a key." The front door was padlocked, but there was no reason for it. Many of the window coverings were torn off or loose, providing easy access to anyone who wanted to get in. "Be careful," he warned as they stepped through the door.

The interior was much worse than he remembered. The walls were marked with graffiti and peeling paint, and the floor was dusty and littered with trash. As they walked from one cavernous room to the next, Dex snapped photos with a digital camera, trying to imagine what the place had been like years ago.

"They called it a convent, but it was really more like an asylum or even a prison for most of the women living here. Fallen women, who were forced to work in the laundry. That was in a building that's gone now, but they lived and slept here, I think."

"Fallen women?" Marlie murmured. "What does that mean? Prostitutes?"

"At first it meant prostitutes, or women who were unmarried and pregnant, or even the daughters of fallen women. The hard work in the laundry was meant to provide rehabilitation, but as time went on, it was a

place to imprison and punish women deemed 'impure.'
And believe me, that label was liberally applied in Ireland. It included the mentally ill and the handicapped,
even abused girls. And later, if a girl was deemed too
flirtatious or promiscuous, she could end up here, too."

"That's horrible," Marlie murmured. She rubbed her
arms, and Dex took her cold fingers and pressed them
between his palms.

"In 1993, the church sold one of the buildings that
had housed a Magdalene laundry in Dublin, and as the
new owner was excavating, they found the remains
of 155 inmates buried in an unmarked cemetery on
the property. That started a huge investigation that revealed the truth about these places, the truth about
how the girls and women were abused. It was a national scandal."

Marlie stared at her surroundings. "Aileen could
have ended up here."

He drew a deep breath. "I think she was here," Dex
said. "I think she spent time here and didn't want anyone to know."

"But I've read the manuscript for her autobiography and she doesn't mention anything about this place.
She talks about growing up in an orphanage under Sister Bernadette and how she learned to read and write
there."

"But there's a gap. Between the time she was fifteen and eighteen. She's covered it very well, but her
story doesn't quite track."

"Track. What does that mean?"

"It doesn't make sense. It doesn't fit the time line."

"How can you be sure?"

Dex stared down into Marlie's eyes, watching as emotion flickered through the green depths. "Claire discovered it first. Ian gave her the manuscript for Aileen's autobiography and she thought the story about Sister Bernadette sounded familiar. So Claire did some digging. She discovered that Sister Bernadette became a bit of a radical and a reformer. When the orphan girls at Lady of Mercy turned thirteen, they were sent to the Magdalene laundries to work. Sister Bernadette saw what was going on and wanted to change it, but she couldn't do that from within. So she left the Church, or was forced to leave, and tried to help from the outside. But she was up against the Church and the government, a force she couldn't fight, and eventually they drove her from Ireland. She lived and taught in London for the remainder of her life, eventually writing a book that's taught at many universities. That's what Claire remembered."

"But surely if Aileen had been at this convent, she would have mentioned it. She's been so truthful about everything. Why would she leave this out?"

"I don't know. Ian believes that after all these years, she's blocked it out. Maybe it was just too painful to talk about."

"But we should be able to prove her story is true. She became a governess. Some of those family members might still be alive."

"I think that much is true. Somehow, she was able to escape this place and start life again. Claire wonders if Sister Bernadette helped her."

Marlie shook her head, then began to pace back and forth in front of him, her feet kicking up dust from the scarred floor. "I know why you brought me here," she said. "You want to ask Aileen about this. You want to include it in the film."

"It's important, Marlie," Dex said. "And yes, we should include it. We should bring her here."

"No!" Marlie said, stunned by his suggestion. "No, no, no. She's a frail old woman, Dex. You can't do this to her. You can't ambush her like that."

"I wouldn't ambush her. We'd talk to her about it first. But I want to bring her back here and get her reaction. To hear her tell us about this place."

"You don't even know she was here," Marlie said. "You're just guessing."

He reached into his jacket pocket and pulled out a photocopy, then handed it to her. "This was copied from the book Sister Bernadette wrote about her years as a nun. Read it."

Marlie stepped over to a window and held the paper in a shaft of sunlight. Dex waited, knowing that the proof of Claire's theory would be difficult for Marlie to accept. Hell, she hadn't wanted to ask Aileen about a simple love affair; she'd never want to bring this up.

"It doesn't mention her name," Marlie murmured, looking up from the paper.

"Bernadette probably wanted to protect the girl's identity. But the story is almost the same story that Aileen tells, down to the detail about *Jane Eyre*."

"Maybe that was Bernadette's favorite book."

"Marlie, you have to admit that this is enough for us

to at least ask the question. She may refuse to answer, but we have to ask. It's our job."

"No," Marlie said.

He grabbed her hand and pulled her closer. "You know it is. We're required to find the truth. It's why we make documentaries. We document the truth. If I didn't want to do that, I'd be making movies in Hollywood and living the posh life."

He watched as she considered his request. This was always the most difficult part of making documentaries, being able to stand back and watch the truth unfold in front of the camera, to not interfere with what was real. Dex had seen many sad and terrible things through his lens, and he'd had trouble on numerous occasions putting those things in perspective. But the world needed to see them.

"I—I have to get out of here." She pulled out of his grasp and hurried back to the door, her footsteps echoing in the cavernous interior. Dex let her go, knowing that nothing he said would change her mind. He'd never compromised on the integrity of a film before. But, damn it, he'd never expected it would come down to this.

Just how far was he willing to go to stand up for what he believed in? This need to show the truth was part of who he was as a filmmaker. It was there in every single film he'd ever done. And now he was actually considering compromising just to keep the woman he was bedding happy.

He cursed softly. If only it was that simple. Marlie wasn't just a one-night stand or some bit of stuff that might be around for a week or two. He had feelings for her, feelings that were growing stronger every day. Hell, it wasn't a leap to believe that he might be falling in love with her.

So what was more important? His professional ethics or her happiness? It wasn't a choice Dex thought he'd ever have to make. A few weeks ago, choosing the woman would have been laughable. But Marlie had changed him. Dex just wasn't sure it was for the better.

MARLIE OPENED HER eyes to the dim light of the bedroom. Her naked body was tangled in the sheets and she wriggled back, searching for the curve of Dex's warm body. But his side of the bed was cold and empty.

She groaned softly, burying her face in the pillow. Things had been tense between them since their return from Cork earlier that evening. In order to maintain the peace between them, Marlie had told him she'd consider his proposal. But she could see what this was all costing him. By ignoring the twist in Aileen's story, he would force himself to compromise—and all because of her.

Maybe she wasn't cut out for this. Maybe she'd made a mistake. It had all seemed so simple, making a film about the life of her favorite author. But Dex had shown her that this was no business for dilettantes. If she wanted to produce great documentaries, then she would have to stand for integrity and honesty.

And yet she couldn't bring herself to hurt Aileen. She was a sweet woman who had never done harm to anyone. She'd entertained millions of women with her stories, giving them strong and honorable heroines to emulate. No one would ever know that they'd left something out of the film. To her, protecting Aileen Quinn was the most ethical thing to do.

She'd tried to bridge the distance between them with sex, but his absence from the bed spoke volumes.

She sat up and looked around the room, then grabbed one of Dex's T-shirts from the end of the bed and pulled it over her head. A decision had to be made. They were due to interview Aileen tomorrow afternoon and if they were going to ask the question, it needed to be done soon.

She found Dex at the table, wearing just his boxers, a glass of whiskey in his hand. The old suitcase of his grandmother's was open on the floor beside his feet. Claire had delivered it last week, but Dex had put it aside when their schedule got busy.

She stood behind him and wrapped her arms around his shoulders, resting her head against his. "What are you doing out here?"

"Just going through some of my grandmother's things."

"Can't you sleep?"

"No. I had a lot of stuff on my mind."

"Me, too," she said, circling around him. She bent forward and touched her lips to his in a soft, sweet kiss. "I'm sorry."

"You don't have to be sorry," Dex said. "I think you're right. We should just let it go."

Marlie sat down on his lap, drawing her legs up against his chest. "And I think you're right. We should at least ask the question. If she refuses to answer or sticks to her story, then we'll let it go."

"My sister told Ian about this. Maybe he should be the one to talk to her first. He's helping her with the book. If he gets her to put it in the memoir, then we could use it in the film."

"He does know her much better than we do. He's been working with her for almost a year."

Dex nodded. "He'll be at the shoot tomorrow. We can talk to him then."

"Agreed." She sighed. "See? That wasn't so bad. We managed to make a decision that we're both happy with."

He slipped his hands around her waist. "I guess I shouldn't be surprised that we argue. Matt and I used to get into some ridiculous rows. I was usually the one with the kamikaze attitude and he was always more… diplomatic. I guess that's why it worked so well."

"I appreciate that you have things to teach me. And I know that I sometimes don't seem grateful, but I am. And I am listening."

Dex slipped his arms beneath her legs and stood up, then carried her back to the bedroom. He tossed her on the bed, flopping down beside her on his stomach. "You shouldn't back down," he said. "I need you to be exactly who you are. That's the only way this will work."

"Even if you don't agree with me?"

"Especially if I don't agree with you."

She smiled at him. "All right. That sounds reasonable to me."

He flipped over and rolled her on top of him, weaving his fingers through hers and pinning them above his head. "Let's seal that agreement with a kiss."

"Then kiss me," Marlie ordered. "And make it good."

A playful growl rumbled in his chest as he dragged her into a lazy kiss. His teeth teased at her lower lip until she opened to his tongue. He tasted like whiskey, and the kiss sent a flood of warmth coursing through her body.

His shaft, now growing hard, pressed against her belly and she shifted against him until he groaned in protest. Marlie loved the sense of power that she had over him, the ability to make him desperate to move inside her. Emboldened by that power, she traced a line of kisses across his cheek to his shoulder.

Pushing up on her hands, she moved lower, using her lips and her tongue across his smooth chest. When she paused over his nipple, flicking at it with her tongue, Dex groaned, trying to pull his hands from her grasp.

He finally got loose and furrowed his fingers through her hair, pulling it away from her face so he could watch her as she continued down the length of his body.

When she reached the waistband of his boxers, Marlie glanced up at him and smiled. "Why are you wearing these?"

"Why are you wearing that shirt?"

Marlie got up on her knees and pulled the T-shirt over her head, tossing it aside. It seemed so natural to be naked with him. Though she'd always been a bit self-conscious about her body, it hadn't been an issue with Dex. Maybe it was because he was Irish and didn't have the same notions of beauty that many American men did.

He loved her curves and told her that her breasts were luscious. And when she saw desire in his eyes, Marlie believed what he said. She was beautiful. And her imperfections were perfectly fine with him. Maybe that was what it was to be loved, she mused. Perhaps Dex was exactly the kind of man she ought to love.

Dex skimmed the boxers over his hips and kicked them off. Marlie ran her nails along his torso, from his chest to his belly, then wrapped her fingers around his shaft. Her lips closed over the tip and she began to seduce him with her mouth.

Marlie had always felt rather clumsy about this part of sex. She'd never been comfortable that she knew what she was doing. But she and Dex hadn't been shy about communicating in bed. Unlike the other men she'd been with, she told him exactly what made her feel good. And he reciprocated, urging her on when she found a tantalizing technique.

She ran her tongue along the length of his shaft and teased at the tip. Dex gasped, his hands twisting in her hair. He gently pulled her back, but Marlie ignored his signals and continued to tease him toward release. As he always did to her, she brought him closer to the edge, then allowed him to relax, knowing that his orgasm would be more powerful that way.

And when she'd worked him into intense anticipation, Marlie found a condom and smoothed it over his erection, careful not to send him over the edge with her touch. All along, he'd watched her through passion-glazed eyes, which continued to follow her as she straddled him.

He grabbed her hips and held her away until he'd regained a measure of control. But Marlie didn't want to wait. She *wanted* him to lose control, to need her so much that his body betrayed his mind. Grabbing his shoulders, she pulled him up, wrapping her legs around his waist.

Marlie barely moved, shifting slightly against him as they lost themselves in an endless kiss. And then he was there, a moan slipping from his throat as his orgasm overwhelmed his control. She smiled to herself, cupping his face in her hands as she continued to kiss him.

This man had become such an important part of her life in such a very short time. It didn't seem possible that this was all happening to her, that she'd found someone who could make her feel so alive.

Though she knew her time in Ireland was quickly coming to end, she couldn't imagine ever leaving Dex behind. How would she live without him? Would every man she met pale in comparison? Or would she come to regret their brief affair?

Marlie was practical enough to realize that not every sexual relationship ended in true love. But it felt right to believe in the possibility, especially with Dex.

7

DEX DROPPED THE pizza on the table, then shrugged out of his jacket. "Dinner," he said to Marlie. "You'll love it. Best pizza in Killarney. And I had to drive like a madman to get it here while it was still hot."

"I'll eat pizza hot or cold," Marlie said, scooting her chair over to open the box. She wore an old shirt of his, unbuttoned to reveal a tantalizing view of her cleavage, and a pair of his boxer shorts. Her hair was pulled back in a haphazard ponytail and she'd put a pair of his wool socks on her feet.

"I think it's still warm."

"I am starving." She opened the box, then looked up at him. "There's a piece missing."

"I got hungry in the car. You try driving twenty-five kilometers with the scent of pepperoni pizza wafting through the car. You and pizza. The two things that destroy my self-control."

"So do I rank above or below the pizza?"

"Oh, way above," he said. Dex wandered over to the

fridge and grabbed a beer, then twisted off the cap. He took a long drink, the refrigerator still open. "Hello, Mr. Guinness. Perfect end to a perfect day."

"If we're going to be living here, Dex, we probably should buy some food and try cooking a few meals every now and then."

"Are we officially living here? Because if we're going to spend every night sleeping in the same bed, we should move into your room at the hotel. They have room service, don't they?"

"Yes, but the walls are thin and we can't make as much noise as we make here."

"Point taken," he said. "Tomorrow, we'll fetch your things and bring them over. And we'll put the money we're saving back into the production budget."

"Speaking of production, I'm still worried we're not going to be ready when all her relatives come into town. They'll be here in two weeks and we've still got so much to do. I don't want it to seem as if we're imposing or taking time away from their holiday, so I want to be as efficient as possible."

Dex grabbed a piece of pizza and took a bite. "Don't worry about those interviews. We're not going to use a lot of that footage. I just want to make sure we go back to the Magdalene laundry. Did you talk to Ian about that today?"

Marlie nodded. "He still hasn't found the right time to bring it up. He said he and Claire want to do some more research. I think he's worried Aileen might believe we're accusing her of keeping something from us."

"Perhaps he's too close to her. Maybe you need to say something."

She took a bite and nodded. "I'm supposed to meet with Claire and Ian tomorrow while you're filming exteriors at her house. We'll come to a decision."

He grinned at her. "Good girl. See, you're starting to think like a producer."

"I had a great teacher." She took another bite and groaned. "This is really good."

Dex sat down across from her and she popped up from her chair. "I want a beer, too." But as she moved toward the kitchen, she stumbled over the suitcase that he'd set next to the table over a week ago.

Marlie cursed and hopped up and down on one foot as she rubbed her toe. "Why is that suitcase still here? I've stubbed my toe twice on it." She picked it up. "Where does it belong? And why did you ask Claire to bring it back?"

"No reason," he said. "It was just a crazy idea I had."

She came back to the table with a bottle of beer and sat down. "What was it?"

"When you showed me that photo of Conal, it seemed familiar. I remember when I was younger, my grandmother used to sit in that chair over there with this suitcase on her lap and go through these old photos. And I thought I'd seen that photo of Conal in her collection." He chuckled. "Now that I've said it out loud, it sounds crazy."

"No," Marlie said. She set her beer down and picked up the suitcase, laying it on the end of the table. She flipped the clasps and opened the bag. It was filled with photos, some of them old and tattered and printed in sepia tones. Others were more current, taken at holidays and birthdays that Dex remembered. "Maybe we should go through these."

"I'm sure it's just a photo that resembled the one of Conal. Some other guy in a British army uniform."

"God, wouldn't that be something if your grandmother had known Conal? Maybe we should look. Stranger things have happened."

"Go ahead," Dex said. "While you look, I'm going to eat some pizza."

Marlie took a sip of her beer and began to rummage through the photographs. But her search was interrupted each time she came across an old photo of Dex.

He sat down beside her and they laughed over his skinny body and long, shaggy hair. There were photos of his parents when they were young, and his grandmother as a child. Though he'd never known his grandfather Kennedy, he recognized the photos.

One by one, they examined every photo in the suitcase, but none of them came close to resembling the photo of Conal.

"Are there any more?" Marlie asked after she'd packed the photos back into the case.

"Yeah. But you've got things to do. I'll put this away and we'll go through more another night. Nana's stuff isn't going anywhere."

"You're right. I'm just trying to avoid working on this script. I can't seem to edit myself. If I don't learn how, this documentary is going to be four hours long."

"All right, once I put this away we'll work on the

script." Dex grabbed the suitcase and walked back to his grandmother's bedroom. He flipped on the bedside lamp, then glanced around the room. Not much had changed since Nana's death. Her clothes were still hanging in the closet and all her treasures and memories were scattered around the room. He picked up her wedding photo and stared into the face of a young woman who looked very much like Claire.

But Dex couldn't get the notion that he'd seen Conal's picture before out of his mind. And now that they'd started looking, he didn't want to stop.

Dex set the frame back in place and opened the closet door. A shelf above the clothes held shoe boxes filled with greeting cards and old letters. He set the suitcase on the floor and grabbed an old photo album, opening it to the first page.

His heart stopped as he recognized the face from Marlie's photograph. He quickly flipped to the next page and the same man was there again, standing with Dex's grandmother, his arm around her shoulder. Each page held a different photograph and then, there it was, the portrait of Conal, dressed in uniform.

"Jaysus," Dex murmured. He hadn't imagined this. He *had* seen this photo before and then tucked the memory away in a corner of his mind.

He pulled the photo from the album and was surprised to find an inscription on the back. "For my Dee, with all my love, C."

He gulped in a breath as he did the math in his head. His father had been born in 1949, so his grandparents must have been married at some point before that. His grandmother had been born in 1925, so she would have been in her early twenties when she knew Conal.

But Conal had been born before Aileen. He would have been in his thirties during the war years, maybe even older.

"What are you doing in there?" Marlie called. "If you don't hurry up, I'm going to finish this pizza by myself."

Dex shoved the album back onto the shelf. He'd look at it later, after Marlie was asleep. He wasn't sure why his instincts urged him to keep it a secret for now, but Dex had learned to trust his instincts. He wouldn't tell Claire, either.

Ian could keep this secret, though. He'd know what to do. Dex closed the closet door and turned off the light, then returned to their dinner. Marlie was sitting on the edge of the table, her shirt unbuttoned down the front.

In that moment, Dex forgot all about his discovery and turned his attention to the beautiful woman in front of him. "What are you about?"

"I'm hoping you don't notice that I've eaten more than half the pizza." She pushed her shirt aside to reveal her naked breasts. "Look. Boobs."

"You're in Ireland. The proper word is diddies." He stepped in front of her and grabbed her hips, pulling her against him. Dex ran his hand up the length of her leg, then bent and flicked his tongue over her exposed nipple. "I'm very, very angry about the pizza."

"What are you going to do about it?" Marlie asked, tipping her head back as he sucked gently.

When he'd brought her nipple to a peak, Dex moved to the other side. "I think a spanking might be in order."

"Really? A spanking? I *am* a naughty girl." In the blink of an eye, Marlie slipped away from him, running around to the other side of the table. "But you're going to have to catch me first!"

Dex ran around the table, only she was quick and managed to stay ahead of every move he made. She grabbed another piece of pizza and ate it as she scurried around the room, taunting him with it.

He finally caught her near the sofa, wrapped his arms around her waist and pulled her down onto the overstuffed cushions. She lay on top of him and held the slice of pizza in front of his mouth. He snapped at it and she pulled it away, taking another bite.

"Tell me what you want," she teased. "And say please."

"To hell with the pizza," Dex said, his hands skimming down to her backside. "I want you."

She fed him a bite. "You'd better eat now and build up your strength. I plan to keep you up very late tonight."

Dex chuckled as she continued to feed him. He hadn't believed he could be any happier, but with each day he spent with Marlie, things only got better. Sure, they had their disagreements, but they were minor compared to the sweet times they shared.

He never considered the end, even though he knew she'd have to return to the States. But now he couldn't imagine ever letting her go. He wanted Marlie in his life. He needed her. He wasn't sure he could be happy without her.

They had a few more weeks of filming and then another month or more of editing. There was still time to sort that all out. But he wasn't going to waste a single moment with her. He was going to make every minute count.

CLAIRE RIFFLED THROUGH the papers in her portfolio and pulled one out. "Here they are," she said, holding out the stack of photos. "I had him photograph them with some things around them, and then on just a plain background. I think they look much better than scans, don't you?"

Marlie looked at the photos of Aileen's book jackets. "They're beautiful," she said.

"Thanks. Ian suggested the photographer. He's brilliant."

"The photographer? Yes, I'd say so."

"Him, too," Claire said. "But I was talking about Ian."

Marlie glanced up at Dex's sister and noticed a pretty blush coloring her cheeks. She was surprised. Claire didn't seem to be the type to be embarrassed about anything. "He is kind of cute, in a geeky way."

"Yeah," Claire said. "I mean, I've always preferred the footballer type. You know, big and muscular and kind of dumb. But Ian is just so bloody sexy, I want to rip off my knickers and have a go every time I look at him."

"Are you sleeping with Ian Stephens?" Marlie asked.

"Don't you dare tell Dex. He would kill me. I mean it."

Marlie bent closer. "I won't tell him."

"I don't begrudge Dex his pleasures with you—and don't try to deny it. It's written all over his face. By his blissful expression, I'd say you two have been shagging like bunnies."

"We have," Marlie said.

Claire covered her ears. "I don't want to hear the details. My twin brother and I are close, but not that close." She reached out for another sandwich.

Sally had prepared lunch for them all while Aileen retired to her bedroom for a short nap. Marlie had decided that she'd talk to the author about the Magdalene laundry that afternoon.

"We should go out, you and me and Dex," Claire said. "To a pub. Maybe do a little dancing."

"Dex did teach me how to dance," Marlie said. She thought back to that night at the pub…and everything that had happened after that.

"And if you and Dex come, I can probably get Ian to come. He can be kind of stuffy and I want to loosen him up a little bit. He'd probably have a lot of fun."

"I don't know what Dex has planned for the weekend, but I'm up for it."

Claire smiled. "Good. I'm really glad you and Dex are together. You make a sweet pair."

It was the first time that Marlie had ever thought of her and Dex as a couple. Yes, they were lovers and friends and coworkers, but she'd always seen them as two separate individuals.

"We're really not a couple," Marlie said. "I mean,

not in that way. We're just…" There wasn't a word for it. "We're together. For now."

"Don't hurt him," Claire said. "I'm not sure he could take much more loss in his life right now."

Marlie shrugged. "I don't think he's looking for anything serious. After he's done with his film, he'll go back to his life. He'll find another partner and he'll move on."

"You could be his partner," Claire suggested.

"I'm just a novice at this. And I wouldn't know how to produce the kind of stories he wants to tell. I wouldn't be much use fighting off drug lords in the Colombian jungle."

"Maybe he wouldn't do those kinds of films if you were his partner," Claire said.

Marlie saw the emotion in the other woman's eyes and she realized how worried Claire had been over her brother. Marlie had never had that kind of relationship with any of her siblings. In truth, she felt closer to Claire than she did to either one of her own sisters. "Maybe not," she said.

"I see you two are having a proper chin wag." Dex walked into the solarium and plopped down on one of the chairs. "Please don't tell her any embarrassing stories from my youth. I've worked very hard to impress her."

"I won't," Claire said, getting to her feet. "I'd prefer that she stick around for a while. A good long while, if I had my say."

Claire picked up her plate and headed out of the room. Marlie smiled at Dex, then picked up the plate of ham sandwiches. "Are we going to be able to film outside?"

"Nope. It looks like we're going to get rain. But maybe tomorrow."

"Claire wants us to go out tonight. With her and Ian."

Dex frowned as he considered the request. "Claire and Ian. As in, together? The two of them? Bloody hell, is she shagging Ian Stephens?"

"How do you get shagging from us going out to a pub? Maybe she just wants to have a few pints and relax."

"Don't deny it, I can see it in your face."

Marlie clapped her hands to her cheeks. "You can't see anything in my face!" She grabbed her linen napkin and held it in front of her. But Dex snatched it from her fingers.

"Sure," he said. "We can go out. In fact, I've been anxious to have a little talk with Ian. So has my fist."

"Why are you upset? You can sleep with me and it's all right, but she can't sleep with Ian?"

"She's my sister. And she hasn't a very good history with men."

"I'm someone's sister, too. Although I'm not sure either of my brothers would leap to my defense."

"It's different," he murmured, taking a bite of the sandwich.

"How?"

He stared at her as he chewed and Marlie waited for his answer. At first she didn't think he had one. But then she realized that he had an answer, he just didn't want to say it out loud. "You're the guy who's always talking to me about truth," she said. "So give me the truth. Why is it different?"

He set the sandwich down and brushed the crumbs off his fingers. "Because this isn't— Our relationship isn't just about sex. You're not some bit of skirt to me."

"What am I?"

"You're special," he said. "You're different than the others." He grabbed another sandwich and stood up. "We're going to talk to Aileen about the laundry this afternoon. It's time."

She drew a deep breath. "I know. I'm ready."

Marlie watched him as he walked away. She leaned back in her chair and thought about what he'd just told her. She was different. Special. What did that mean?

Until now, she hadn't really been concerned about defining their relationship, but suddenly she wanted to. How did he feel? Beyond the physical attraction, was he hoping they might have a future together? And if he did, how did he imagine that would work? Would she live in Ireland? Or would he live in Boston?

Groaning, she rubbed her hands over her face. This was so much easier when she didn't think about the future. Perhaps there would come a time when they had to make a decision about their relationship, but why worry about it now? They needed to finish the film first.

Marlie got up and walked back through the entry hall. Aileen was already in the library, dressed in the same dress she'd worn for all the interviews. Marlie quickly went through her continuity checklist, making sure her earrings were on right and her hair was styled the same way. When she was finished, she sat down in her chair.

Dex stood near the camera, but he hadn't turned on the lights yet. Aileen looked over at him expectantly. "Are we ready to start?"

"Actually, there's something we need to talk about before we begin," Marlie said, gathering her resolve. "We've come across something in our research." If Aileen didn't want to talk about it, then she could simply refuse. "We found a book written by a woman named Sister Bernadette. She talks about an orphan she helped, an orphan who was sent to live at the Good Shepherd Convent and then to work at the Magdalene laundry. Aileen, was that you? Did they send you to that place?"

Aileen's hand trembled as she brought it up to her lips. In that instant, Marlie wished she could take it all back. But she couldn't. She glanced over at Dex and he gave her an imperceptible shrug.

Time seemed to drag on as Aileen focused her attention outside the library window. Finally, she spoke. "The day I walked away from that horrid place, I vowed I'd never let it enter my mind again. It was three years of my life that I willed myself to forget, and until now, I'd done a good job. Even when the scandals about the Magdalene laundries were in the paper, I convinced myself that none of that was about me. It wasn't part of who I became. But maybe it is time to talk about my experience."

She waved at Dex to turn on the camera. Marlie

quickly got up and switched on the lights, and when Dex nodded, she began. "When and why were you sent to the Good Shepherd Convent?"

"I was fifteen," Aileen said, her voice remarkably clear and strong. "Sister Bernadette had been giving me extra paper so I could write as much as I wanted. She'd been sneaking me romantic novels from the library, and when one of the older nuns searched my room she found my romance stories. The nuns read them and thought they were sinful. They asked me where I'd gotten the books but I refused to tell. By that time, I'd decided I wasn't going to take the vows, but I hadn't told them that because I didn't want to lose my place at the school. I was already teaching some of the younger children, and it was really the only home I'd ever known. But then because of a few stories, they sent me to the Good Shepherd laundry, and for the first time in my life, I realized that hell might actually exist on earth."

THE MUSIC IN the pub was lively and loud. Dex and Marlie and Ian and Claire had enjoyed a late dinner there after leaving Aileen's, then had gotten caught up in the growing crowd that came for the band.

Dex leaned over the bar and grabbed Marlie's hand, giving it a kiss. "Ian and I are going out to get some air. We'll be back in a few minutes."

"We'll come with," she said.

"No, you stay here. You girls are always sneaking off to the loo together. We need a little man time."

Marlie gave him a knowing look and grinned. "All right. But be nice."

Dex tapped Ian on his shoulder and motioned him to the door.

As they walked out into the chilly night, Ian shoved his hands in his pockets and glanced at Dex uneasily. "Listen, I know why you brought me out here, and I want to reassure you that my intentions toward your sister are strictly honorable. She's a wonderful woman and I think I might be in love with her."

Dex gasped. "What? What the hell are you talking about?"

"Didn't Marlie tell— But Claire said— Oh, bollocks." Ian turned away and walked a bit down the pavement in front of the pub, rubbing his hand through his hair. He stopped short and walked back, his expression contrite. "I apologize. I assumed you were aware that Claire and I have been seeing each other. She told me that Marlie knew, and I figured Marlie would have told you."

"Of course I know. You're shagging my sister. It's the other thing that concerns me."

"What?"

"You're in love with my sister?"

"I realize I'm not really her type, but we seem to get on quite well, and I find her enchanting."

"My sister, Claire, is enchanting?" Dex shook his head. "That word isn't usually applied to Claire. But I guess, as my father always says, there's a nut for every bolt."

Ian forced a smile. "Yes. Well, I think we can agree that Claire would be the nut."

"Sure. But she's my twin nut, and I hope that you don't break her heart."

"I have no intention of doing that." He rubbed his hands together, his breath clouding in front of him. "Can we go back inside?"

"No, there's something else I wanted to talk to you about. Come on, I have it in my car."

They walked down the street to where Dex had left his SUV. Ian hopped in the passenger side and Dex slid in behind the wheel. He started the BMW and turned on the heat, then grabbed his bag from the rear seat. He pulled out the old photo album and handed it to Ian.

"What's this?"

Dex switched on the light above the rearview mirror, illuminating the interior. "Open it," he said.

Ian did as he was told and held the scrapbook up to the light. Perplexed, he slowly flipped through the pages. When he reached the copy of the army photo, he stopped. "Bugger and blast. It's him. It's Conal Quinn. Where did you get this?"

"It belonged to my grandmother."

"Please tell me she's still alive," he murmured.

"She died three years ago." Dex paused. "I want you to take that and figure out what it means. And don't say anything to Claire. Or to Marlie. Until we've figured it out, it's just between us."

"Why the secrecy?" Ian asked.

"My father was born on February 16, 1949. My grandparents were married on September 8, 1948.

Count it out. My grandmother was pregnant when she married my grandfather. And if you look at that first photo in the book, it's dated June 1948. My grandmother and Conal Quinn were together nine months before my father was born."

"Bloody hell," Ian murmured. "This isn't some kind of joke, is it?"

"No."

"If your father is Conal's son, then that means—"

"Yeah. I know. And that's why, until we figure this out, we need to keep it quiet."

"There's an easy way to prove your theory. Take a DNA test. We've checked all the heirs to make sure they're who they say they are. I have a lab I've been working with."

"All right," Dex said. "The sooner I find out the better. If I am Conal Quinn's grandson, that's going to affect the film."

"How?" Ian asked.

"I can't continue to associate myself with it," Dex said. "I'm part of the story. I've stepped through the wall. The film will lose all credibility."

"So what will happen?"

"I'll find someone else to finish it. And I suppose I'll have to appear in it. It does kind of add an interesting twist to the story."

"That's a massive understatement," Ian said.

"But until then, take that back to your car and don't let Claire see it."

"All right. See if you can find more. Letters, cards, anything from that period in your grandmother's life."

"That's going to be difficult with everything we're doing on the film. But I'll try."

Dex turned off the ignition and they both hopped out of the car. He waited while Ian ran to his car, then they reentered the noisy pub. Marlie and Claire were still in the same spot at the bar, but two young bowsies had taken Dex and Ian's spots beside them.

Dex stepped up behind Marlie and kissed her neck. She spun around, then smiled in relief when she saw it was him. She put her hands on his cheeks. "You're cold."

"Warm me up. Come on. Let's have a dance."

He took her hand and led her to the crowded dance floor. But just as they got there, the rowdy song the band had been playing finished and the band began a slow ballad. Dex pulled Marlie into his arms, holding her hand close to his chest.

It felt right to hold her close, to feel the warmth of her body against his, to inhale her scent. She'd become such an important part of his life; everything had changed so quickly and so drastically since he'd met Marlie.

And now it might change again. If what he suspected was true, he was about to inherit a rather considerable sum of money.

He couldn't even bring himself to consider it. Hell, if he'd wanted to be rich, he would have been working in Hollywood all along. It had always been about the work for him. But with that kind of money, he could finance his own film. Or he could choose to sit on a beach for a few years getting a suntan.

"Claire," he murmured. She'd inherit, too. And so would his father. This could change everyone's life.

Marlie drew back. "What?"

"Nothing," Dex said. He smiled down at her, then brushed a kiss across her lips. This could all be nothing but a coincidence. He couldn't let himself think about it now. He had to focus on Marlie and the film they were making together. That was more important than any inheritance.

But even as he tried to put it out of his mind, Dex knew, deep down, that his theory was the truth. His father wasn't a Kennedy, he was a Quinn. And Dex was a Quinn. And when he came face to face with all those Quinns at the reunion, he'd be meeting his new family.

The song came to an end and he stood on the dance floor, holding on to Marlie. "Are you all right?" she asked, stepping back to look up at him.

"No," he said. "Let's get out of here. I want to go home and take you to bed."

He led her back to the bar and they said their goodbyes to Claire and Ian. Then he helped Marlie into her jacket and grabbed his from the back of his stool. When they got outside, he slipped his arm around her shoulders and pulled her close.

"Do you want me to drive?" she asked.

"No, I'm perfectly sober."

"You are," she said. "You only had one pint with dinner."

"I wanted to keep a clear head," he said.

"What did you and Ian talk about?"

"He confirmed that he and Claire were knocking boots."

"That's not a very Irish saying, is it?"

"Matt always used that phrase. He was American."

"Well, even though they are knocking boots, there's nothing you can do about it."

"I'm not sure how I feel about that."

"The same way Claire feels about us being together. She's happy that you're happy."

Dex frowned. "Really?"

Marlie laughed. "Come on. I want to go home and get naked and snuggle up beneath the blankets with you. We've got a busy day tomorrow, and the sooner we get to bed the better."

He opened the car door for her and she got inside. Dex leaned over her and gave her a kiss. "But we're not going to sleep when we get home, right?"

"Oh, I'm sure you can find a way to keep me up."

"And I know that you know how to keep me up, too."

She gave him a playful shove. "That is just about the cheesiest thing you've ever said to me. Is that how you charmed women before you met me?"

"No. But you still love me, right?"

"I sure do," she teased, patting his cheek.

As he closed the door he realized what he'd said to her. It had just come out, without a serious thought to what it really meant. But he wanted nothing more in life than for her to feel that way about him. To hell with the money or the film or anything else that used to matter to him.

Marlie made him happy; she was all he really needed. Without her, he was just the same old Dex Kennedy. With her, he was a man who could do anything.

8

"ARE YOU SURE you're going to be all right?"

Marlie held tight to Aileen's hand. Claire was on her other side and Ian walked ahead, making sure the path was clear.

They'd made the drive down to Cork that morning. Dex had left earlier to scout out a good location inside the orphanage where they could shoot. Since the building didn't have electricity, he was worried about finding a decent light source.

Marlie, on the other hand, was worried that Aileen wasn't up to such a long trip and a stressful day of shooting. But when she'd arrived at the country house early that morning, the writer was waiting in the entry hall, dressed and ready to go.

When they reached the end of the path, Aileen stopped and stared up at the facade. She drew a long breath, then slowly let it out. "I didn't ever want to see this place again." Pressing her hand to her heart, she fought her emotions, and Marlie pushed back her own tears.

"Take your time," Marlie said.

"Come along. It's best to just face our fears, isn't it? It's nothing but an old building. The memories inside it can't hurt me now."

Over the next hour, they filmed Aileen standing near a broken window, the ruins of the orphanage providing a stark backdrop to her interview. She talked with brutal honesty about her memories of the place, about the living conditions and the way she was treated.

Marlie couldn't help her heart going out to Aileen for all she'd had to endure. It was difficult to believe any child could survive what she had and still become a successful, intelligent and kind adult.

Dex was happy with the footage they'd gotten, and thanked Aileen for her patience and her honesty. He walked out with her while Marlie began to pack up the equipment.

But for some reason, Marlie's emotional reaction to Aileen's interview wouldn't fade. She walked into the center of the room and gazed up at the ceiling, closing her eyes and letting the tears fall. When she heard Dex approaching, she brushed the dampness from her cheek and went back to stowing the equipment in canvas cases.

"Well, that went much better than I expected," he said.

"Yes," Marlie murmured.

"I'm glad the weather was decent."

"Mmm."

Dex crossed the room to help her fold up a microphone stand and she moved away to occupy herself with some other task. But he caught her hand and turned her around to face him. "What is it?"

"Nothing," Marlie said. "I—I just got a little emotional listening to her talk about her childhood." She held up her hand. "I know, I know. I should be able to maintain objectivity, but I guess I'm not there yet."

Dex dragged her into his embrace and Marlie buried her face in his shirt, tears flooding from her eyes. She wasn't even sure why she was crying. It was a sad story, but Aileen had lived through it and become a triumphant success.

He smoothed his hand over her hair and whispered soothing words. And when she finally felt better, Marlie looked up at him and smiled. "Sorry. I'm not sure what's gotten into me."

"It's a natural reaction. Don't be ashamed of feeling something, Marlie. I got a little choked up, too."

"You did?"

"Yeah. It's hard not to. She's an amazing woman."

Marlie nodded. "I started thinking about my own childhood. I complain a lot about my family, but I had everything I could ever want or need, except maybe unconditional love. But I was safe, and well fed, and educated in a private school where the teachers were kind. I have no right to complain. It's selfish."

"No, it isn't. There's nothing wrong with you wanting to be loved. Parents should always show their children that they love them."

She took a ragged breath and wiped at her cheeks

with her fingertips. "My parents thought love would make us…soft. That if they withheld love and affection, then we would work harder to gain their approval." A laugh burst from her lips. "You know, it's a wonder I'm not more screwed up than I am. It's a bloody feckin' miracle, it is," she said, laughing.

It felt good to laugh about it. What else could she do? And it felt especially good to laugh with Dex.

"That's a pretty sick way to raise kids. Even though my parents weren't around much, we never had any doubt that they loved us."

She went back to packing the equipment, her heart a bit lighter. "If I ever have children, I swear, I'm going to tell them every day that I love them. And that they're perfect exactly the way they are."

Dex held the case open and she folded a light reflector and put it inside. "You'd be a great mom."

"Do you think so? I don't really know that much about kids. Or babies. I'm not sure I could do it. My mother didn't let us have dolls when we were kids. We had educational toys. We probably could have all been replaced by robots and she might not have ever noticed."

"Don't you have any nieces and nephews?"

"Yes. Each of my siblings has two children. They would have had 2.5, but as smart as they are, they haven't figured out how to do that. I never see my nieces and nephews, though. They have busy lives and my family never really gets together, except for awards ceremonies where there might be photographers. They're not big on holiday celebrations."

"What about Christmas?"

"Everyone goes on a cruise. But I get seasick, so I usually stay home."

The whole story sounded so pitiful, and Marlie didn't want him to think she was seeking sympathy. She'd long ago accepted that her family would never be "normal." But that didn't stop her from wanting to experience Christmas or Fourth of July with people she actually loved and who loved her. "It's all right. They are what they are. At least they're consistent."

Dex gave her a fierce hug. "Come on, let's get out of here. There's somewhere we need to go."

"If you're going to take me to another sad place, I'm going to stay in the car. I can't take any more weeping today."

Dex pressed his forehead to hers, his fingers soft on her nape. "This is probably one of the happiest places in the world. I promise." He kissed on the end of her nose, then followed it with a sweet, tender kiss on her lips.

Marlie's knees went weak, and she wanted to fall into his arms and lose herself in the oblivion of sexual pleasure. But the surroundings were definitely not ideal, and she was cold and her fingers were numb.

So they grabbed the equipment and carried it out to the SUV, Dex making a second trip while Marlie sat in the car and warmed up. She closed her eyes and smiled to herself. Dealing with hurt or disappointment had always been such a solitary exercise in the past. But it was so much better to have someone there who could offer her at least a little sympathy and understanding. It made getting over the bad times so much easier.

Dex tossed the last of the equipment in the backseat and then they were off, heading along the river to the narrow streets of the city center. They crossed over the river and by the time they jumped into a traffic circle, Marlie wasn't sure what direction Dex was driving.

"Here," he said. "I think this is it."

"I hope they have good chips," she said with a sigh. "And very strong drinks. This has been a long day."

"You figure we're going to a pub, then?"

"You said it was the happiest place in the world. I'm pretty sure Ireland doesn't have a Disney World, so what else could it be?"

"Wait for it," Dex said. "It should be coming up." He peered down the street. "Yes, this is it."

He pulled to a stop in front of a huge Christmas tree lot and found a place to park, then glanced over at her and smiled. "They even have a Santa. And he's not drunk."

Marlie laughed. She leaned over him to stare at the riot of lights and greenery. "What are we doing here?"

"We're going to get a tree. You'll be here over the holidays, so I think we should do it up. Christmas with all the trimmings. And that starts with a tree."

Overwhelmed, Marlie threw her arms around Dex's neck and hugged him tight. "You really are the sweetest man I've ever known. And now I'm going to start crying again."

He looked down at her and smoothed his fingers over her cheeks. "Save your tears. You'll need them later. My sister says that I'm impossible when it comes to choosing a tree. It has to be absolutely perfect, and so it usually takes me at least an hour to pick one."

"I think I can bear it."

He hopped out of the SUV, and this time, Marlie allowed him to get her door. He took her hand as she jumped down, and she took the chance to kiss him again, right there on the sidewalk. He pressed her back against the side of the truck, his hands slipping beneath her jacket to find warm skin.

"Or maybe I can settle for a less-than-perfect tree, after all," he murmured against her lips. "We need to get you home and into bed where I can properly warm you up."

Dex PULLED UP in front of the pub, then glanced at his watch. He had about fifteen minutes before Marlie would start to wonder where he was.

Ian had called earlier that afternoon with news that he'd received the preliminary results from Dex's DNA test. Dex had asked him what they were, but Ian insisted on meeting him.

Marlie had been occupied with decorating the Christmas tree they'd bought, picking through the boxes of ornaments he'd carried down from the cottage's attic. So he'd offered to fetch them supper from the pub in the village, then called Ian and asked him to meet there.

Dex hurried into the pub and scanned the interior for signs of the researcher, but he hadn't arrived yet. Dex busied himself with ordering dinner for him and Marlie, then asked the barkeep to draw a half pint.

Ian arrived a few minutes later, and they moved to a table in a quiet corner of the pub. Ian placed a file folder on the table in front of him and cleared his throat.

"First off, I need to tell you that these results are only preliminary. I won't have the final report for another month. But—"

"I'm not a Quinn," Dex said. He felt a flood of relief. Being a Quinn would have made everything much more complicated. Sure, it would have been nice to enjoy a financial windfall, but he was—

"No, you are," Ian said. "All indicators point to the fact that you are the grandson of Conal Quinn and the grandnephew of Aileen Quinn."

Dex stared at Ian, stunned by the news. "There has to be some mistake. What are the odds that this would happen?"

"Ridiculously high," Ian said. "But not astronomical. Ireland is a small country. Almost everyone is related in some way. You're all from the same part of Ireland. Although it is odd that you're making a film about her life."

"Not anymore," Dex murmured.

"You're not going to continue?" Ian asked, frowning.

"Someone else will have to. I can't. It's a documentary, and I'm now part of the story. I've lost my objectivity."

"But that shouldn't matter. Who better to make a film about Aileen than one of her heirs? I remember Prince Charles made a film about the queen."

"And everyone knew that he wouldn't reveal the

complete truth. Quitting at the moment I learned the truth should be enough to save the integrity of the film. And I have a friend in mind who can finish it. He'll just have to do the interviews at the reunion and get a few exteriors, once we get some decent weather. And we were going to hire an editor, anyway, so we should still be able to finish on schedule." Dex drew a deep breath. "I'm going to have to tell Marlie. She won't be happy."

Ian passed him the folder. "I did some additional checking and it does appear that your grandmother was pregnant with your father when she married your grandfather. She was at least three months along, so she would have known. I can't say whether Marcus Kennedy knew. He might have lived his life believing that the child was his. I suppose we'll never be sure. Once the DNA test is complete, though, I'll have all the proof I need to make you an official Quinn."

He stood up and held out his hand. "I hope you change your mind about finishing the film." Ian turned and walked toward the door, then stopped and came back to the table. "By the way, I'm going to ask your sister to marry me on Christmas Eve. I've bought a ring and I plan to ask your father for her hand, but I suppose I ought to ask for your blessing, too. Since you are her twin brother."

"You only met her what, three weeks ago?"

"Well, I did get to know her on the phone when I was trying to find you. So it's actually been about six weeks. I realize it's not long, but when you feel it's right, there's no reason to waste time."

Ian stood silently until Dex realized he was waiting

for an answer. "Go for it," he said. "I'm not sure she'll say yes, but you won't know until you ask."

The other man smiled warily, then nodded. "Very well. I'll see you soon."

By the time Dex finished his beer, his food was ready and packed in a paper sack. He paid the barkeep and headed back out. Any other bloke would be jumping for joy at the sudden financial windfall. But in truth, his mind wasn't on his good fortune. It was on how the news might affect his relationship with Marlie. The documentary had been the glue that was holding them together. Without that, they'd be forced to define how they felt about each other.

Hell, he knew exactly how he felt. It had been pretty clear for days now that he was in love with Marlie. She'd brought him out of the darkness and into the light again. But Dex also realized that in order to have a future with her, he would have to fundamentally change who he was. He couldn't love Marlie and return to his profession.

As he drove home to the cottage, he turned it over and over in his head, trying to find a way to have both. This was what Matt had always told him—it was impossible to have it all. You had to make compromises. He could still be a filmmaker, he'd just be a different kind of filmmaker. The kind who made films about famous authors.

Dex slipped in the front door and smiled at the scent of pine in the cottage. Marlie had finished decorating the tree. She'd turned the lights down and found a few candles to add to the festive atmosphere. Christmas music played from the radio. She looked up from the sofa at the sound of the door.

"Hey," she said with a warm smile. She got up on her knees, resting her hands on the back of the sofa and gazed at the tree. "What do you think?"

"Beautiful," he said, keeping his eyes fixed on her face.

"I saved the star on the top for you. And we can plug in the lights together after we eat."

He shrugged out of his jacket and brought the take-away over to the sofa. "Why don't you unpack this and I'll get us something to drink?"

"I have wine," Marlie said, pointing to the open bottle on the floor at her feet. "Grab a glass for yourself and some plates."

When he was settled in beside her, she handed him a plate and scooped some of the stew onto it, following it with a piece of black bread.

Dex studied her silently. She seemed so happy here with him, as if she'd found a place to belong. What if he asked her to stay forever? Would she? Or was she already thinking about going home?

"I just had an idea about the script," she said, digging into her stew. "What about if we took some excerpts from Aileen's books and wove them into the story? I can recall so many things from her books that are based on her life. And that would give the viewer a sense of who she is as a writer that you wouldn't get otherwise."

"That's a brilliant idea," Dex said.

"Really? I wasn't sure if you'd like it. I was afraid it

might slow down the pacing. But then again, if we're showing something interesting on screen, maybe it won't. And—and maybe we could get Aileen to read the excerpts."

Dex turned and set his plate down on the arm of the sofa. Reaching out, he slipped his arm around Marlie's nape and gently drew her closer. His lips found hers and he kissed her, lingering for a long time over her mouth.

"Are you trying to seduce me?" she asked, a naughty smile curling the corners of her mouth.

"No," he murmured. "I guess I just wanted to enjoy my dessert before the main course."

She sighed. "You know, we have to start thinking about editing. After this weekend, we'll have finished shooting. And I was hoping we could put together a little teaser film that I can send back to Boston to give them an idea of what we're doing."

"We could do that. There's a guy I use in Dublin. He does a lot of our editing."

"It's going to be good," she said with a smile.

"Yes, it is." He paused, considering his next question. "So when do you think you'll be going home?"

She seemed surprised by the question, then frowned. "I haven't made any plans. I guess I'd like to stay until we're done editing, if that's all right."

Dex searched her expression for some sign of regret or doubt, but she seemed to be resigned to the fact that they'd say goodbye in the not-too-distant future. He considered telling her now, revealing the startling news that Ian had brought him, but it could wait. If she was headed back to Boston soon, he wanted one more night of this.

"I think we make great partners," Dex said.

"I think so, too," Marlie replied, smoothing her fingers over his temple. "Who knows, maybe we'll work together again sometime."

They finished their dinner, and Dex threw a few more blocks of peat on the fire before returning to Marlie.

"So what is Christmas like here in Ireland?" she asked, snuggling up against him.

"Well, there's the tree. And we usually put a holly wreath on the door. And we wear awful Christmas jumpers—sweaters to you. And, oh, the biscuits. I'm not sure why this is, but there's a type of biscuit that everyone buys at Christmas. They're called USA biscuits."

"Like Christmas cookies," she said.

"Yeah, only they come in a tin, and you can't break through the paper to the bottom layer until you eat all of the biscuits on the top." She gave him an odd look and Dex laughed. "Yeah, I know. It doesn't really make sense. We also read James Joyce's short story 'The Dead.' It's kind of the Irish version of the Grinch. What do you do?"

"Well, we never did the Santa Claus thing because my parents thought it was harmful for their children to believe in fantasy creatures and imaginary holiday icons. So we didn't have the Easter bunny, the tooth fairy, ghosts and witches at Halloween or leprechauns on St. Patrick's Day."

"No leprechauns?" Dex sighed dramatically, shaking his head. "You did have a horrible childhood."

"I know," Marlie said. "We did get gifts from our parents at Christmas, but they were never wrapped. And they were always very practical. I remember one Christmas, I got a fountain pen, a globe and an anatomy textbook."

"Well, I'm sure we can make your Christmas much better this year," he said. "Let's light that tree up."

Marlie clapped her hands and jumped up from the sofa. She dragged him to his feet and they stood in front of the tree. "The star first," she said, pulling it out of a plastic bag.

Dex took it from her and placed it on the top of the tree, then bent down to find the cord for the lights. He plugged it into the wall and the tree instantly blazed with blue and gold and red and green. The smile on Marlie's face was priceless, and he stepped back to her side and wrapped his arm around her waist. "Nice tree," he murmured.

"It is," she said.

"You know, there is one other Irish tradition I didn't tell you about. It's called the tree-lighting shag."

She sent him a sideways glance, her eyebrow arched quizzically. "Oh, yeah. And what's that all about?"

"Well, after the tree is plugged in, we strip off all our clothes and chase each other around the room until someone gets caught. And then there's very hot, very passionate sex."

Marlie reached for the hem of the T-shirt she wore.

"All right." She tugged it over her head, revealing her naked breasts. Then she skimmed her pajama bottoms off and kicked them aside. "Now you."

When Dex was completely naked, she gave him a nod. "Ready?"

"Set," he said.

"Go!"

She screamed as he reached for her, but managed to elude his grasp. Marlie ran around the sofa a couple of times, Dex hard on her heels. But then she took a detour into the bedroom and jumped onto the bed. Dex crawled on top of her and braced his weight on his hands, their hips pressed together.

"I think I've been caught," Marlie murmured, staring up at him. She pulled her leg up along his thigh, then ran her foot down his calf. "Let the shagging begin."

As Dex began a slow, deliberate seduction, he knew that this was exactly what he wanted. He didn't care what he had to give up to make it happen, but Marlie was going to be with him next Christmas, and the Christmas after that and every Christmas for the rest of their lives.

MARLIE SAT DOWN on the bed and pulled the top off the paper coffee cup. She held it close to Dex's nose, and a few seconds later he opened his eyes. His long, muscular legs were tangled in the bed linens and he tugged at the sheet until he could free himself and sit up.

"What a nice way to wake up," he said, raking the hair out of his eyes.

"I figured you'd enjoy it," Marlie said. "I have pastries, too. And I bought eggs and sausages and bread for toast. Oh, and orange juice. I'm going to make us a big breakfast. We'll call it the post-tree-lighting-shag breakfast."

"I like it," Dex said. "And maybe part of the tradition could be you cooking breakfast wearing just an apron and a Santa hat?"

"I think you'd be happy if I spent all my time in this cottage naked." She tossed a paper bag at him. "Eat your pastry."

He caught her hand before she could walk out and pulled her back down onto the bed. "Share this with me," he said. Dex opened the bag and tore the cheese Danish in half, then handed a piece to her.

Marlie pulled her legs up on the bed, crossing them in front of her. "What's on the schedule for today?"

He hesitated before he spoke, and Marlie sensed he had something to say that she didn't want to hear. She'd learned to read the signs—the tiny furrow in his brow and a half smile were usually followed by a suggestion that she do something differently.

"What did I do wrong?" she asked. "Just spit it out, we'll argue about it and then I'll make breakfast."

"No," Dex said. "It's not that." He cleared his throat, then reached out and grabbed her hand. "Yesterday, Ian brought me a bit of news. I haven't said anything to you about this because I wasn't sure it meant anything, but now I know it does. I told you that I thought I recognized that photo of Conal. It turns out I have seen it before, in my grandmother's photo album. My grandmother knew Conal Quinn."

She gasped. "Oh, my God," Marlie said. "And you told Ian about this? Has he been able to find Conal?"

This was amazing. Of all the luck, to find Conal's descendants just days before the family reunion. "This completes the story," she said. "But I don't understand why you wouldn't have told me."

"Conal had a son. A grandson and a granddaughter." Dex drew a deep breath. "Marlie, my father was Conal Quinn's son."

At first, Marlie wasn't sure she'd heard him right. His father? But that didn't make sense. How could his father be the son of—? "I don't understand."

"Conal Quinn got my grandmother pregnant, but instead of marrying him, she married Marcus Kennedy. She was about three months along when they got married. So I'm the guy Ian has been looking for. Or at least one of them. My father, me and Claire are related to Aileen Quinn."

"You're going to inherit," she murmured, her eyes wide.

"Yeah," he said.

Marlie giggled. "Do you realize how weird this is? What are the chances? I mean, if I hadn't involved you in the film, or if Ian hadn't found that photo of Conal… You're sure about this?"

"We did a DNA test. The results aren't completely final yet. That's why we're not telling anyone—not Claire or Aileen. If it is a mistake, I don't want them to be disappointed."

"When will you find out?"

"Three or four weeks. Unless we uncover other proof." He wove his fingers through hers. "There's something else."

"How could there be something else?" she asked.

"And this is the hard part. Now that I'm connected to the subject of the film, I can't be the producer anymore. I have to stop working on it."

She frowned, searching his expression. He had to be teasing her. Dex had just found out he would inherit a million dollars and he was going to quit working on their film? But try as she might, Marlie couldn't see any trace of humor in his expression. "You're going to quit?"

"Marlie, I have to. I can't be behind the camera *and* be part of the story. It will ruin the film's credibility. I've already called a friend of mine who will finish up the filming and work with you on the script, and it will be great. Then the film goes into editing."

Marlie shook her head. "No. You can't just quit. Everyone arrives in three days. We made an agreement. You have a responsibility to me. I can't do this on my own."

"I have a responsibility to your film first. And you can do this. You don't really need me. You know exactly what you want and what's necessary for the film."

Marlie got up from the bed and wandered back into the living room, trying to digest everything that he'd told her. How could this be happening? They should be celebrating his good fortune, not worrying about their work.

She sat down on the sofa and buried her face in her hands. This would change everything. Without Dex attached to the project, how would they market the film? Would the distributors and the film festivals still be interested, or would the film go straight to video and barely get noticed?

She sat up. Doing this on her own was frightening, but she wouldn't give up on her dreams. Besides, it wasn't as if Dex would be working with her on her next film, or the one after that. She'd have to sell those on her own—she'd sell this on her own, too.

"Are you all right?"

She felt his hands on her shoulders and Marlie nodded. "Yeah. I can do it. It won't be as much fun, but we're almost done. We just have to film interviews at the reunion and record Aileen's voice-overs." She reached for his hand. "I just wish you could be there to finish it with me."

He circled around the sofa and sat down beside her. "It's going to be a great film whether I'm there to finish it or not. It's already good. Besides, now you'll get to interview me."

"And I'll see you at night, won't I?"

Dex gave her hand a squeeze. "That's got to change, too. At least until you're in postproduction. If you want, you can stay here and I'll move back in with Claire."

"What about Claire? She's working for us—I mean, me."

"She's pretty much done the research. And I think her mind is on other things—like Ian Stephens. We're not going to say anything to her until we've got the final DNA test, so it's important that you don't tell what we know."

Marlie sat silently, the ramifications of all this beginning to sink in. She'd grown to depend on Dex, to seek his opinion, to revel in their relationship. And now it was just going to stop.

"Maybe this is for the best," Marlie murmured. "I'm going to have to go back home soon. And it's going to be hard enough to leave. A little space might be a good idea."

For a long time, Dex didn't speak. Marlie wanted him to object, to tell her that she belonged in Ireland with him. But even if he asked, she realized she wasn't really ready to accept. She needed to return to Boston, needed to take her film with her and make sure it found a place. And she needed to make sure she repaid her grandmother. Then maybe she could think about her future.

"What are you going to do with all that money?"

Dex shrugged. "I don't know. Maybe I'll invest in your next film?"

A laugh burst from her throat and she followed that up with a groan. Marlie flopped down onto the cushions. "I'll go back to the hotel in Killarney," she said. "You can stay here."

"You'll be in postproduction by Christmas. We'll still spend Christmas together. And New Year's, too."

Marlie curled up against him, wrapping her arms around his waist. "How am I going to do this without you?"

"You'll have two weeks. You'll survive."

"What about Aileen? Are you going to tell her?"

"Not until we're sure. But I'm going to spend some time going through my grandmother's things to see if I can find more proof. Hopefully we can tell her before the reunion."

"I think Aileen is going to love welcoming you as a Quinn. It will be wonderful for her to have someone right here in Ireland."

"A Quinn. It's strange to discover I'm not really a Kennedy."

Marlie kissed his cheek. "I'm going to make breakfast and then we're going to spend the rest of the day in bed. I don't care if I get zero work done. If we're going to be apart for the next few weeks, I need to have plenty of fantasy material."

Dex kissed her, cupping her face between his hands. "You're going to miss me. You won't have anyone to argue with."

He didn't have any idea the depth of her fears and insecurities. But it wasn't only the film that she was worried about. They had something very special together, and Marlie wasn't willing to concede that it might be coming to an end.

"Claire is going to freak out about this," Marlie said.

"Not as much as she's going to freak out when Ian asks her to marry him."

Marlie pulled back. "Hold the phone. When did you find out about this?"

"Last night. Ian asked my blessing. I didn't say anything because I didn't want to tell you I'd met with him.

Not until I figured out how I was going to tell you everything else."

"You're just full of interesting tidbits," she said.

"Feed me breakfast and I'll give you all the details."

9

THE COTTAGE WAS silent, the only sound coming from the wind outside and the crackle of peat in the hearth. Dex walked to the kitchen to grab another beer from the fridge, then wandered back to the sofa.

The floor was covered with boxes that he'd pulled out of every storage space in the cottage. He'd never realized how sentimental his grandmother was. She'd saved pictures that he and Claire had drawn when they were very young children. She had packed away greeting cards and interesting recipes and photos from her favorite magazines. But though he'd been searching for most of the day, he hadn't found anything else about Conal.

It was a relief to have something to occupy his thoughts. Marlie had been gone for two days. She'd been working on finishing the shots with his friend and fellow filmmaker Dan O'Meara. He'd lined up Flannery Carr to do the editing and had checked in with Ian to make sure everything was going well.

His mind spun back to their last few moments together, just before she'd left the cottage. She hadn't been happy, but she'd been willing to listen to him about what was best for the film. Now that she was gone, Dex had reason to question his judgment.

Hell, he could have finished shooting. He could have done the work and then just refused to put his name on the film. They could have continued on. He could have still been able to see her every day. The only rule he would have been breaking was one of his own making.

He reached for his phone and checked it. He and Marlie hadn't spoken since she'd left, but that didn't stop him from hoping she'd call. He'd been tempted to send her a text, but then realized that she needed to triumph on her own.

Though he wanted to believe there might be a future for them, he couldn't be certain. And if there wasn't, then she needed to walk away from this experience ready to make a success of her career.

Dex took a sip of his beer and grabbed another shoe box, this one tied with a striped ribbon. He tugged it off and opened the box, only to find it filled with more letters. But as he pulled a packet from the box, he caught his breath.

There was a military return address. He slid one of the letters from the envelope and quickly scanned the contents. It was a letter from Conal.

Over the next several hours, Dex read every letter in the box, close to one hundred of them, tied into little packets by year. Six years, starting in 1942 and ending in August 1948.

The letters outlined a love affair that began with a chance meeting between Conal and Dierdre. She'd taken a job in Cork as a hotel maid and met him at a dance one night. That first meeting had begun a secret love affair. Conal had been trapped in an unhappy marriage, unable to divorce a wife he didn't love.

As he read the letters, Dex scribbled notes, important points that he wanted to convey to Ian. This was all the proof they needed. They'd be able to tell Aileen before the reunion dinner and the Kennedys would become part of the Quinn family.

He smiled to himself. Marlie would be happy. She had the perfect ending to her film, the descendants of all four brothers coming together to make a family for Aileen.

His thoughts were interrupted by the sound of the door opening. The moment Dex heard the squeak of the hinges, his heart jumped and he hoped to find Marlie standing in the doorway. But his sister was there instead.

"What the hell is going on?" she demanded. Claire slammed the door behind her. "Did you quit?"

"No," Dex said. "Well, yeah, but not the way you think."

"What is all this?" She pointed to the mess on the floor. "Is this Nana's stuff?"

"Sit down. Can I get you something to drink?"

"No," Claire murmured. "Well, maybe a whiskey would be good. Did you and Marlie have a fight? She told me you walked away from the film."

"I have. I can't work on the film anymore."

"Why not? Bloody hell, Dex, why would you desert her now?"

"Because I'm going to end up *in* the film. So are you. And Da, too, if he can come home for Christmas."

"What are you talking about?"

Dex carefully explained the story to his sister. As he laid out the facts, she listened, her eyes wide, an astonished expression on her face. Dex was happy to be the one to tell her that her financial worries would now disappear. She worked so hard as a teacher, and now she'd have financial security.

When he was finished, Claire silently got off the sofa, retrieved the bottle of whiskey and took a gulp right out of the bottle.

"Jaysus," she murmured. "Mary and Joseph, too. I don't know what to say."

"Claire Kennedy with nothing to say. Did hell just freeze over?" Dex teased. He grabbed the bottle and took a drink, then handed it back to her. "Who would have figured the Kennedy twins would come out millionaires."

"A million euros?"

"Give or take. I'm not certain of all the details. I didn't want to ask questions before I was sure."

"How long can you live on that kind of money?" she asked. "I wouldn't have to teach. I could go back to school, I could write a book. Oh, my God, I could travel. I could go everywhere I ever wanted to go. I could even buy a trip to the space station if I wanted to."

"Since when have you wanted to go to the space station?" Dex asked.

"Never," Claire replied. "The point is, I could."

"I could finance a film," Dex said. "On a subject I really want to explore. Or maybe a subject Marlie wants to explore."

Claire twisted around to face him, her fingers clutching the bottle. "You're in love with her."

It wasn't exactly a question. More like a statement. And faced with Claire's certainty, Dex had to nod in agreement. "Yeah, I'm pretty sure I am. We've been apart for three days and I'm bloody banjaxed. I don't know which way is up, and I want to call her, but I can't bring myself to risk rejection."

"I understand how you feel. Last night, Ian asked me to marry him and I said yes." She winced, shaking her head. "Don't scold. I realize we only met a month ago, but when you know, you know. You know?"

"I thought he was going to wait until Christmas," Dex said.

"He told you?"

"Yeah, he asked my permission."

Claire sighed. "Oh, that's so sweet. He's just so… sweet." Groaning, she buried her face in her hands. "I can't believe I've fallen for a guy who irons his boxer shorts."

Dex threw his arm over Claire's shoulders. "Now that we have money, we could both move back to Hollywood and become beautiful and glamorous."

"I like my life here," Claire said. "What are you going to do about Marlie? How are you going to convince her to stay?"

"I have no idea. Maybe I'll go with her, back to Boston."

"You can't leave me," Claire said.

"You have Ian now," he said.

The answer seemed to pacify her and she leaned her head on his shoulder. "Isn't life strange?"

"Stranger than strange," he replied.

As they finished off the whiskey, Dex mulled over the possibility of leaving Ireland to follow Marlie to Boston. He'd lived all over the world in all kinds of conditions, so why was it such a difficult choice to make? Was it because he was making it for love and not for work?

Taking a professional risk was part of the business, but he'd never risked his heart. But nothing good in his life had ever come to him without a bit of fear and trepidation. Dex suspected that Marlie would be no different.

MARLIE STARED AT her reflection in the mirror, worrying at a strand of hair that refused to stay in place. Of all days to have a bad hair day, this was not the one. She hadn't seen or talked to Dex in almost a week. And in that time, her entire world had changed.

Without Dex, she'd had to find her courage and confidence. They'd finished the script and begun recording the voice-over. She was making all the decisions now, using everything that she'd learned from him. And though she reached for the phone at least ten times a day, Marlie knew exactly what he would say if she asked him a question. This was her film. She was the boss.

She gave her hair a final check, then drew a deep breath and walked out of the bathroom. They were filming the reunion interviews at the castle that Aileen had rented for her guests. It was a perfect place to film, full of beautiful backgrounds.

They'd spent a long day recording the thoughts of all of Aileen's relatives from other countries, and now they'd come to the Irish branch of the family. Dex and Claire were waiting, ready to answer Marlie's questions. She smoothed her hands over her skirt, trying to get rid of the clammy feeling. When she touched him for the first time, she didn't want him to know how nervous she was.

It seemed as if they'd been apart forever. At least during the day she could deal with the loss of his professional expertise. But at night, there was no way to replace his sexual talents. Bed was no longer an adventure in experimentation. Instead, she tossed and turned, plagued by memories of what they'd once shared.

Was this what love was all about? Exhilarating highs and depressing lows? Marlie had never expected this overwhelming melancholy. She felt so lonely and pathetic. The only thing that came close to brightening her day was thinking about the wonderful time she'd spent in Dex's arms.

"Marlie?"

She looked up to find Dan standing in the doorway. "Right. I'm ready."

He smiled. "I'll just give you two a few minutes."

"Two?"

"I think it would be good to film Dex and Claire separately at first, and then together. And Ian just grabbed her and dragged her away. So it's just Dex."

"Right," Marlie said. "All right. Give me a few minutes."

Dan walked past her and Marlie drew a deep breath. She couldn't let Dex see how much she'd missed him. For the next few hours, she had to act like a detached observer, a professional who could separate business from pleasure.

She walked in the room to find him watching interview footage on the monitor. Her gaze skimmed across his muscular back and then drifted lower. A shiver skittered through her and she drew in a sharp breath.

Dex turned around and Marlie's heart stopped for a moment. He smiled. "You caught me," he said. "Sorry."

"No, no. It's fine. What did you think?"

He shrugged. "It doesn't make a difference what I think. What did you think?"

"They're good. Some of them are really good. The guy from Australia, Logan, was very funny and charming. And Jack, from America, was polished. He does a lot of work on camera. And Rourke from… Where was he from? Nova Scotia, I believe. Anyway, he was very reserved. It was hard to get him to talk. And now there's you."

"And Claire. I'm not sure where she is."

"She's with Ian. We're going to do you alone first."

"Do me?" He grinned. "All right. I can handle that."

Marlie took a few more steps into the room. Nothing

had changed. He was still the same charming, playful man she'd grown to love. "You know what I mean."

"Of course I do. I was just wondering if you remembered."

"I do," she replied in a breathless voice.

He took a few steps closer, his gaze fixed on hers. "I've really missed you."

"And I've missed you," she murmured.

"And right now, all I can think about is kissing you."

"Me, too."

"And touching you."

"Me, too."

He reached out and took her hand, hooking his finger through hers. But then he reconsidered and drew his hand away, shoving it in his pockets. "Sorry, you need to focus on this interview," he said. "Not...you know."

"Of course," Marlie said, trying to maintain her composure. She closed her eyes and took a deep breath. "Why don't you sit and relax and I'll just go find Dan."

"He'll be back," Dex said. "I told him to give us a little time. So how is it going?"

"Great. We've started editing and that's going well. And we went to the Good Shepherd orphanage and got some more footage. Aileen wanted to make another trip. She's decided to write a book about her experiences at the Magdalene laundry. And I'm flying home day after tomorrow to present the project at a big public broadcasting meeting in New York. I've managed to build some buzz about the project there and they're all anxious to find out more. They're looking at it for their literary-masters series next spring during pledge season."

"That's fantastic," Dex said.

"And we've got a distributor here who wants to do a big premiere at some art house in Dublin. Plus we've got the film festivals. That could change everything. The publicist at Back Bay is working on that for me."

"It sounds like you have everything under control," Dex said.

Marlie felt a flush warm her cheeks. "Not everything…obviously." She swallowed hard. "I know we made plans to spend Christmas together, but I'm not sure if I'm going to be back. If the national broadcaster likes the preview, they're probably going to want me to stick around. And Flannery isn't going to be available for editing between Christmas and New Year's anyway, so it might be good to get some work done at home."

"Sure," Dex said. "I understand."

Marlie tried to read his thoughts, but he didn't reveal a clue as to his feelings. Was he simply pretending that he didn't care, or had he resigned himself to the fact that their "future" was quickly coming to an end?

She sat down in the chair across from him. "Have you talked to Aileen yet?"

"She invited Claire and me for tea last week."

"Did she mention that you might have more cousins? Ian has tracked Conal to New Zealand. His first wife died, but he remarried and had two more kids, so there's a good chance there are more Quinn cousins."

They stared at each other for a long moment and Marlie searched for another topic of conversation. It had never been difficult to talk to him in the past, and now they could barely communicate. Everything had changed, and not for the better.

"Your tie is crooked," she said.

Dex adjusted it, but it still wasn't quite right, so Marlie stood and bent over him, her fingers working at the knot. He looked up, and for a moment, the world stopped spinning and she stopped breathing. His lips were so temptingly close, just inches from hers, and Marlie knew that if she just moved a few millimeters, it would be all over. They could go back to the way things were.

But then Dex moved his gaze away and Marlie realized he wasn't going to give in. He was determined to keep things strictly business for now.

"Are you ready?"

They both glanced over at Dan, and Marlie straightened. "His tie was crooked," she said. "It's fine now."

"All right," Dan said. "Let me just adjust our lighting and we can start."

Marlie stared down at her notes and tried to calm the hammering of her heart. If she could just get through this interview, then everything would be fine.

Luckily, once she began the questions, her instincts took over and she forgot all about her earlier unease. Dex had filmed so many interviews that he almost anticipated her questions, and he was always ready with a quick answer. The interview went on much longer than the others, and by the time she posed her very last question, Marlie was exhausted.

But she had no chance to recover, or to think about

everything that hadn't been said. Dex walked out of the room and Claire came in next, and Marlie began all over. But this time, it was like interviewing a good friend. She was funny and bright and her answers about what she planned to do with her inheritance were wildly irreverent.

"All right," Marlie said after a quick half hour. "Let's bring Dex back in and we'll—"

"He left," Claire said.

"He left?"

She nodded. "He asked me to tell you that everything was fine and he'd talk to you soon. I think he was worried that he was a distraction." Claire sent her a sympathetic smile. "It's always about the work with him. I'm sorry."

"No," Marlie said. "He's right. It is a little tricky to navigate with him here. And we don't need to interview you together." She sat back in her chair. "Everything is so mixed up. I don't know how to feel anymore. It all made sense when we were together, but maybe I was just imagining how good it was."

"How do you feel about him? Really feel?" Claire asked.

"I wish I could say. I have to go home the day after tomorrow, and I'm almost glad to go because it will put an entire ocean between us. And maybe I won't be constantly thinking about calling him and seeing him and—"

"I'll just go get something to drink," Dan murmured.

When they were alone, Claire leaned forward and took Marlie's hands. "I'm not going to tell you what to do. I'm not going to give you advice. This is between you and Dex. But if you do decide that you love him, I'll be very happy that you'll be in his life—and mine, too."

"Thanks," Marlie said, tears threatening to spill from her eyes. She quickly stood. "I'll let you get back to Ian. And congratulations on your engagement. I'm so happy for you."

Marlie hurried out of the room and searched for a private spot to have her breakdown. She found a small sitting room off the main hall and slipped inside, just barely getting the door closed before she broke into sobs.

This was crazy. She felt as if her entire life had spun out of control—and over a man! This couldn't be what love was about, this ridiculous emotional roller coaster. She couldn't live like this. Things had to be settled.

She brushed the tears away with her fingertips and cursed softly. "Stop it," she muttered. "Just get a grip."

"Is everything all right?"

Startled, she glanced around the room and found Aileen sitting in a wing chair near the fireplace. "I'm sorry, I didn't mean to interrupt."

Aileen waved her hand. "Don't be silly. Sit. I just came in here to get away for a moment. This can be a bit overwhelming for a woman my age."

Marlie walked over to the fireplace and took the chair next to Aileen. "It's a wonderful party. Everyone is so happy to be here for you."

"I hope so. And I hope it isn't just about the money. I'm not trying to buy a family, I just want all my hard

work over the years to mean something. I want someone to remember me when I'm gone. At least for a little while longer."

"You will be remembered. I'll remember you. I
didn't tell you before, but one of your books changed
my life. I was thirteen and I found *The Days of Mary
Larrimore* at the Boston Public Library. The librarian
almost didn't let me check it out because she didn't
think it was appropriate for a girl my age, but that
only made me want to read it more. I took it home and
couldn't put it down. I didn't sleep for an entire weekend. The heroine was my age at the beginning of the
book and she was all alone in the world, which was
exactly how I felt. But she triumphed in the end. And
I knew, from that moment on, that I'd be fine. It didn't
matter if my family didn't understand me. Someday,
I'd find someone who did."

"All that from one of my books," Aileen said.

Marlie nodded, wiping away a fresh round of tears.
"A story like that can change a person's life."

"And what is your story now? Why are you hiding
your tears here, all alone?"

"I'm just a little confused and frustrated."

"I assume Dex is the reason?"

She drew a ragged breath. "Yes."

"Then let me give you a piece of advice. You can
take it or leave it, as you wish. Don't ever leave anything unsaid. The words that you're afraid to say are
usually the most important." She slowly stood, her pale
hand gripping her cane. "I'm old. You should listen to

me." With a soft chuckle, she walked out of the room, leaving Marlie to her own thoughts.

It was good advice. But did she have the courage to follow it?

MARLIE GLANCED AROUND the conference room at Back Bay Productions, nervously toying with the remote control for the video player. Everyone had gathered to see the ten-minute promo that she and Flannery Carr had put together. It was the perfect teaser, carefully crafted to get everyone excited about the film. And from the expressions on everyone's faces, it was doing the trick.

When the promo came to an end, she stopped the player and flipped on the lights. "So that's it," she said. "I know you're disappointed that Dex Kennedy isn't going to add his name to the credits, but now you can understand why."

"Actually, I don't," Kevin Mills said.

Marlie turned to her boss. "Dex has built a reputation in the film industry and he didn't want to compromise that, or compromise the reputation of this film. Once he became part of the story, he felt it was necessary to step away as a producer. But as you can see, his fingerprints are all over this film. I learned so much from him."

The head of programming for the Boston-area public-broadcast station spoke up next. "When can we expect to air this?" Antonia Carson asked.

"Well, we're hoping it might be shown in some theaters first. And of course, Ellie already has feelers out for all the major film festivals. We'll do pay-per-view and a DVD. But I hope it will be available to you in about eighteen months."

"And if you don't get theater distribution?" she asked.

"I fully intend to make sure this film is seen in theaters," she said. "We have a distributor lined up who specializes in art films, and we plan to hold a premiere event in Dublin as soon as we're ready to release it. Aileen Quinn has promised to attend."

"Well, I'm sure I speak for all of us when I say that we're looking forward to seeing the finished film," Kevin said.

"We are very interested," Antonia said. "I'd like to take the promo to our big network meeting in March. I'm sure the response will be favorable."

"Great," Marlie said. She shook Antonia's hand and then said her goodbyes to the rest of the attendees, graciously accepting their compliments and trying to maintain her excitement.

The meeting couldn't have gone better. Unless Dex had been there at her side. Even now, talking about the film, it was difficult to ignore his contribution.

"Congratulations, Marlie," Kevin said.

"Thank you," Marlie replied.

"It's not often that a first-time producer gives us something this good."

"Well, I can't take credit for all of it. I had a lot of help."

"I realize we're up against the holidays here, but I'd like you to meet with our marketing team after

Christmas and put together a plan. If the film is going to be finished as soon as early February, we need to get moving."

"Actually, I'm headed back to Ireland tomorrow evening," Marlie said. "I've got to finalize the script and we've still got to get through editing."

"Maybe we should bring the editing back here and have our people do it."

"No," Marlie said.

"It would save money," Kevin said. "It makes sense."

"The film needs to be edited in Ireland, by an Irish editor. I think that's important and I won't have it any other way."

Kevin chuckled. "Well, you certainly know your own mind, don't you? I like that in a producer. So when you come home, we're going to make it official. You'll be a producer here at Back Bay. And we'll want some ideas about your next project."

Marlie waited to feel elated at his news but strangely enough, she was indifferent. There was no rush of excitement, no sense of pride. She'd waited years to become a real producer, to claim that title, and now that it was within her grasp it didn't really mean anything. It was a title and nothing more.

Dex had shown her that what was important was the work, the people she met, the stories she told. She didn't care about a nice office at Back Bay or a bump in salary. All Marlie wanted was to make great films. And she wasn't sure she wanted to do that here in Boston.

"We can talk about that when I get back," Marlie

said. "I have a lunch scheduled with my mother and grandmother now."

"Well, please thank her again for her investment in this film. I'm sure she'll be happy to know that her faith in you has paid off."

"Yes, my grandmother has always hoped I'd find my own success in the world." Marlie grabbed her things and nodded at Kevin. "I'll keep you in the loop as to when to expect the finished film."

She hurried out of the conference room and grabbed her coat and briefcase from the small cubicle that was once her office. Looking at it now, she wondered how her world had ever been so small.

She rode the elevator down to street level, then grabbed a cab to travel the seven blocks to the restaurant. She was already ten minutes late and her mother had no tolerance for tardiness. But her grandmother would at least understand that Marlie had important work to do while she was in town.

As she strode into the restaurant, she spotted her mother and grandmother seated at their usual table. Her mother was dressed in Chanel, a dirty martini sitting in front of her. Her grandmother appeared no softer. Simone Simpson Jenner was an imperious woman, the kind of socialite who wielded her considerable power with both grace and wit.

Her expectations for her children and grandchildren were high, and she didn't mince words when it came to expressing her disappointment. A trait she must have passed along to Marlie's mother.

"Hello, Grandmother, Mother," she said, sliding into the chair across from them.

"You're late. I'm on my second martini," her mother replied.

"Well, then, it's good that I'm late. You're usually much easier to take after a few drinks."

"Don't be impertinent," she chided.

Simone grabbed her reading glasses from her purse and slipped them on, peering at Marlie with a shrewd look in her eyes. "What's different about you?"

"Nothing," Marlie said. She reached in her coat pocket and handed her grandmother the promo DVD. "That's a sneak peek of our film. I think you're going to like it, Grandmother. It's turning out quite well."

"Then I'm going to recoup my investment?"

"Yes, I believe you will."

"You seem...happy."

"I am happy," Marlie said.

"Why?"

"Because all my dreams are coming true."

"All this over some silly film?" her mother interrupted. "It's not as if you've discovered a cure for the common cold, which I might add, your eldest brother is working on. Did you know that he just got a grant from the National Science Foundation? I'm throwing him a little reception the day after Christmas at the house. I expect you to be there."

"I can't," Marlie said. Suddenly, her family's approval didn't mean anything. Just as with Kevin's approval, Marlie was...indifferent. "I'm going back to Ireland."

"Ireland? Whatever are you doing there?"

"That's where I've been for the past two months," she said. "Filming the documentary. The one Grandmother funded."

Her mother waved her hand. "Oh, I don't want the details, Marlena. All your brothers and sisters are going to be there. There'll be a photographer."

"Mother, I'm through with family photos. Think of how much simpler it would be not to have to explain to everyone why I never went to medical school. And I have someone waiting for me in Ireland, someone who is very important to me."

"Who could be more important than family?" Simone asked.

"His name is Dex," Marlie said, smiling to herself. "And he is just…amazing. You probably wouldn't like him, Mother. He's a filmmaker and I'm hoping that I get another chance to work with him."

"Is this a romantic relationship?" Simone asked with a smile.

"Yes," Marlie said.

Her mother withdrew her BlackBerry from her purse. "Then give me his full name. I'll have him checked out."

"No, I've already checked him out, in my own way, and he's just fine." She reached out and picked up the menu. "Enough about him. I'm hungry. I'm going to have the lobster salad. What about you, Grandmother?"

Her grandmother gave her a wry smile. "Well, I don't know about this man, but Ireland has certainly agreed with you. I haven't ever seen you quite so sure of yourself. Did I ever mention that I once had dreams of becoming a photographer? Jackie Bouvier and I used to freelance for the same newspaper. But then I married your grandfather and I gave that up to help him. I'm glad you're going to have a chance to chase your dreams, Marlena."

Marlie reached across the table and covered her grandmother's hand with hers. "Thank you," she said. "And I didn't know you had an interest in photography."

"Neither did I," Marlie's mother said, crossing her arms.

"I have albums of photos at home. I had my own darkroom. I was quite talented."

"I'd like to see them," Marlie said.

"And I'd love to show you," Simone countered. "Perhaps after lunch? And then we need to do some shopping. Even in Ireland, I suspect that coat would be considered unfashionable. You need something better."

"I agree," her mother said, and then surprised her by adding, "Cashmere would be appropriate for a successful producer."

Marlie smiled, and when the waitress appeared to take their order, Marlie requested a martini. For the first time in her life, she felt completely comfortable around her family, and her mother no less. This was cause to celebrate.

DEX PLUGGED IN the lights on the Christmas tree, then turned off the rest of the lights in the cottage. He stood staring at the riot of color, the shiny lights, the sparkling ornaments. His mind drifted back to the day they'd decorated it.

Marlie was still here, like a spirit that refused to leave. There were memories of her everywhere, and he'd done nothing to banish them. Dex walked over to the fire. He'd been supposed to spend Christmas Eve in Killarney with Claire and Ian, but he'd decided at the last minute to stay home. Spoiling Claire and Ian's holiday celebration wouldn't do anyone any good.

From what he'd heard from Ian, Marlie was still in Boston, meeting with her bosses at the production company. He'd hoped that she might surprise him and come back for Christmas, or even give him a call, but midnight was only an hour away. It was time to concede that her feelings for him had cooled.

Hell, he wasn't surprised. It had been an affair based on geographical convenience, and now that they were miles apart, the passion must not seem quite so intense to her.

He flopped down on the sofa and tipped his head back. How many women had he walked away from in the past? Perfectly nice women with interesting careers and exciting lives. He hadn't thought twice about leaving them, because it was always about his goals and his needs.

Now that he'd been deserted, he had a taste of what that felt like. Marlie had made her choice, and it hadn't been him. It was time to suck it up and move on.

Dex's mobile rang and he frantically searched for it. But as he read the screen, he was disappointed to see that it wasn't Marlie, but Claire. He switched the phone on. "Hello. Why are you calling?"

"It's Christmas Eve, you stupid git," Claire said. "And I just wanted to make sure you weren't planning to stick your head in the oven or pull a toaster into the bathtub. The holidays can be hell for the romantically depressed."

"Very funny," he said.

"Have you heard from her?" Claire asked.

"No. And I don't think I will. She would have rung by now."

"I'm sorry," Claire said. "I really thought you two would—"

"I'll let you get back to Ian," he said. "I'm going to ring Ma and Da in a little while. Then I'm going to go to bed and wake up tomorrow and everything is going to be grand."

"Wait. We're going to come into the village for midnight mass. We want you to come with us. Just like we used to do with Nana. We'll bundle up and walk to church. And then afterward, we'll have something to eat and have a little party. I'll bring all the food and drink. You don't have to do anything."

"Claire, I'm really not—"

"I won't take no for an answer," she said.

He raked his hands through his hair and sighed softly. "All right. I'll see you later. Bring whiskey. I'm all out."

Dex turned off the phone, then retreated to the sofa. He had an hour to himself before Claire and Ian showed up. Certainly, he could find a way to pass the minutes without dwelling on Marlie.

His thoughts wandered to Christmas a year ago. He and Matt had spent it in an odd little hotel in Belize. They were prepping for their trip to Colombia and had decided to take a few weeks off to sun and windsurf before heading into the jungle.

They'd spent most of Christmas Eve at the beach, then sat down on the hotel terrace with a bottle of premium tequila and bowl of fresh limes. Dex remembered thinking that life would never be better than at that moment. Everything had been perfect.

He'd been wrong. Life had gotten better. It had gotten worse first, but then a lot better. Because of Marlie. So many moments filled his memory—quiet moments after making love, silly moments sneaking kisses at work and one serious moment when he'd looked at Marlie and realized what it all meant to him.

Dex cursed, rubbing his eyes. How did every thought, even ones of Matt, end up being about Marlie? Was he that besotted that he couldn't focus on anything else?

He turned on the telly and switched to an American football game. The action on the field was enough to distract him for a while, but when he heard a knock on the door, Dex jumped up, thankful that Claire and Ian had decided to come a bit early.

"I hope you remembered the whiskey," he said, pulling the door open. "Because I'm in the mood to get—"

Marlie stood on the front step, a tattered present in her hands, her carry-on at her feet. "Do you have any idea how difficult it is traveling on Christmas Eve? I landed at noon and it's taken me eleven hours to get here. I left Boston yesterday afternoon, then I went to Montreal and London and now I'm here." She held out the gift. "Merry Christmas."

With that, she burst into tears. Dex gently drew her into the cottage, setting the gift on a chair near the door. He helped her out of her coat and then dragged her into his arms, hugging her body to his.

"I wanted this to be perfect. I was going to look so beautiful and I was going to say something terribly clever and you were going to pull me into your arms and kiss me and—"

Dex tipped her chin up and covered her mouth with his. She tasted of tears and breath mints, but he didn't care. She was here. She'd come back, and he wasn't going to let her go. "It's all right," he whispered. "You got the beautiful part right and I got the kiss right. So we're two for three."

She giggled through her tears and buried her face in his chest. "I look horrible. And I probably smell just as bad."

"Come on," he said, drawing her over to the sofa. "Sit down."

She did as she was told and Dex bent over her feet and tugged off her shoes. He sat next to her, then pulled her onto his lap and kissed her again. "Why didn't you call me? I could have come to get you."

"I wanted to surprise you."

"Well, you did that. I'd convinced myself that I was

never going to see you again. I certainly didn't expect you to show up tonight."

"We said we'd spend Christmas together, and I wasn't going to miss it."

Dex smoothed his palm over her cheek. He'd forgotten just how beautiful she was. Though her face was lined with exhaustion and her eyes were watery, he couldn't imagine anyone more lovely. "We did say that."

"But there are some thing we didn't say," she continued, "and I'm going to say them now. I love you, Dex. I'm not sure how you feel, and I'm not even sure I care." She paused. "Wait. Yes, I do care. But that's not going to stop me from saying it. I love you. And I realize we haven't known each other that long, but it's important that I tell you how I feel." She gazed into his eyes. "And—and now would be a good time for you to tell me how you feel."

Dex let the moment sink in. This was it, he thought to himself. The most perfect moment he'd ever lived. Years from now, he'd look back and be able to remember every little detail, from the way her hair fell across her face to the way his heart seemed to skip a beat when he looked at her.

"I love you, Marlie. And I don't want to live without you. I'm glad you came back. Glad because I wouldn't have lasted much longer. I need you in my life and I'll do anything to make you happy."

"Just being with you makes me happy." She brushed away her tears, then glanced around the room. "Your gift. I have to give you your gift."

She jumped off the sofa and searched the room, then spotted the gift on the chair near the door. Marlie brought it to him, placing it on his lap before sitting down next to him. "Open it."

Dex ran his hands over the package, shaped like a large ball. "I have something for you, too. Let me get it." He set her gift aside and retrieved the small bag he'd put beneath the tree.

When they were both settled again, she pointed to her gift. "You first."

Dex smiled, then gave her another kiss, lingering over her lips until he was satisfied that this wasn't all some kind of hallucination. He tore the paper off to reveal a globe. An old globe. It was marked with little lines drawn in pen and a few stickers.

He wasn't sure what to say at first, but then he remembered the story she'd told him about the Christmas presents from her parents. "Is this your globe?" he asked.

Marlie nodded. "I know it seems like a silly gift, but it's exactly what I wanted to give you. When I was a little girl, I used to dream about all the places I'd go and the people I'd meet. But until I came to Ireland and met you, none of my dreams had ever seemed real. I want to see the world with you, Dex. Wherever you are is where I need to be. It's the only way I'll be happy." She reached out and spun the globe. "So where are we going next?"

Dex stopped the globe from spinning and found Ireland, then pointed to it.

"Where?"

"Right about there is County Kerry. There's this little cottage on the Iveragh Peninsula. And inside the little cottage is a bedroom. And inside that bedroom is a comfortable bed that's been waiting for you to return. And in that bed is me. That's where we're going next."

"Take me to bed," Marlie said.

"First you have to open your gift."

Marlie worked at the ribbon on the small box. She removed the velvet case inside, then opened it. With a gasp, she withdrew the ring. "It's a claddagh," she said.

"It belonged to my grandmother."

"And you're giving it to me?"

"She'd be happy to know that I'm happy. I'm not sure, but I suspect Conal might have given it to her. It was tucked away in a box of his letters. Conal brought us together. I think it's time someone wears the ring. Happy Christmas, Marlie."

She gazed down at the ring, then looked up at him. "I love it."

Dex stood and pulled her to her feet. But as they were walking to the bedroom, he heard another knock at the door.

"Dex?"

He groaned, recognizing his sister's voice.

"Is that Claire?" Marlie asked.

"Yes. I promised her I'd go to midnight mass with her and Ian. Maybe if we're very quiet, she'll think I left already and she'll go away."

"No," Marlie said. "I want to go."

"You're not too knackered?"

"I'm exhausted. But it's our first Christmas and I want to experience it all."

Marlie walked to the door and opened it. When his sister saw Marlie, Claire threw herself into Marlie's arms. They laughed and cried while Ian stood quietly behind them. He looked over at Dex and nodded, a content smile brightening his expression.

Dex had lost so much, but it was time for a new beginning. He'd give Marlie the family she'd always wanted, and she'd give him the love he'd never known he needed. His life with the woman he loved would begin tonight.

Epilogue

"IT'S DONE."

Ian stood in the doorway of Aileen's library, a cardboard box in his hands. He entered and set it down on her desk.

"I've entered all the changes and checked every last fact and the memoir is ready."

Aileen reached out and placed her hand on the top of the box. "We've had a long journey together, haven't we?"

Ian nodded. "Thank you for the opportunity. I've really enjoyed working with you."

"I have something for you," Aileen said. She opened her desk drawer and withdrew an envelope. "After all this time, I've come to think of you as part of my family. You were the first one to discover the existence of my brothers, and you helped me find their children and grandchildren. And now you're going to marry my grandniece. So I'd like to make sure that you have the chance to make your life what you've always wanted it to be." She held out the envelope. "I'm giving you an equal share of my estate."

Ian stared at her in disbelief but Aileen waved the envelope at him. "Take it."

"But Claire already has her share."

"And now you have yours. Use it. Go off and write that book you've always wanted to write. Or spend your days doing research. Or help me write my next book about my days at the Magdalene laundry. We'll coauthor it."

"I—I would be honored."

"Take it," Aileen insisted. "Make an old woman happy."

Ian reached out and took the envelope from her fingers. "Thank you. For everything."

"You know, we aren't quite finished yet. We still haven't tracked down Conal's other family in New Zealand."

"I've been working on that. I'm hoping to have some news soon."

"Good. Now why don't you go find Sally and ask her to make us some tea. We'll have a quick cup, and then you can get back to your new fiancée."

Ian tucked the envelope into his jacket pocket and walked out of the library.

Aileen smiled to herself, then reached across her desk and picked up the photograph she'd placed there just that morning.

The image was fresh and colorful. She sat in a chair, surrounded by her family, a family that until a few weeks ago had been scattered around the world. They'd come together for a short time to celebrate a holiday that had always been lonely for her. But that had all changed.

Though she might not have many years left, this would be the Christmas she always remembered. This would be the Christmas when she found her family.

* * * * *

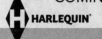

Available December 17, 2013

#779 UNFORGETTABLE
Unrated!
Samantha Hunter

After an explosion leaves firefighter Erin Riley with nearly complete amnesia, she has no recollection of her former lover, Bo Myers, the fire investigator on her case. But their strong attraction is something she can't deny....

#780 TEXAS OUTLAWS: JESSE
The Texas Outlaws
Kimberly Raye

Jesse James Chisholm is back in Lost Gun, Texas, and he intends to do whatever it takes to bring out the bad girl in Gracie Stone before she hangs up her wild and wicked ways for good!

#781 STILL SO HOT!
Serena Bell

Dating coach Elisa Henderson is ready for anything when she accompanies her new client to the Caribbean—anything, that is, except her onetime friend and almost lover Brett Jordan. Suddenly it's not just the island temperature heating things up!

#782 MY SECRET FANTASIES
Forbidden Fantasies
Joanne Rock

I was about to realize my two biggest dreams—opening a shop on the coast, and penning a steamy novel. But the sexy owner refused to sell his property to me. And the hero of my book began to resemble him more and more....

HBCNM1213

REQUEST YOUR FREE BOOKS!
2 FREE NOVELS PLUS 2 FREE GIFTS!

red-hot reads!

"Forget it," Erin said flatly, trying to step around him. "I'm never going back to being a firefighter, ever. We both know it."

The night air lifted her scent. It surrounded him, mixing with the sweet evening aromas of fresh grass and recent rain. Though distracted, he reached out, stopping her again. He knew he shouldn't.

"So now what? What next?" he asked.

They were close. She looked up at him, and the irritation in her face disappeared. Bo didn't know if it was his imagination or wishful thinking, but heat arced between them like it had back in the bar.

Like it always had.

"I don't understand this," she said, stuttering a bit, unsure. Rattled.

"What don't you understand?"

"Why I— What this *thing* is with you."

"What thing would that be, exactly?"

"Why I feel…when we… I don't know you. I don't even think I like you much," she said, shaking her head. "But when I look at you, I…"

She remembered. Or some part of her did.

He took her chin between his forefinger and thumb.

Bo knew he should walk away, call a cab and leave. He should let this be.

But he wasn't going to.

"I think I know what you mean. I feel it, too," he said, his voice a whisper.

Her eyes widened, and without warning she turned her cheek into his palm. The light rub of her skin on his set his blood on fire, and sense evaporated. Everything was lost to the night, except being close to her, finally. Bo wanted to be closer.

He slid his hand back around her neck, bringing her forward until she bumped up against him. Then they were kissing, and it was the first time he could breathe in months.

He thought it would be a quick, gentle kiss, but it came on suddenly, like a summer storm. Her arms wrapped around him and she was pressing into him like she always had, as hungry as he was.

As he explored her throat before working his way up to her lips again, she pulled away, as if suddenly realizing what was happening. At the same time, voices rose in the parking lot behind them.

Bo could hardly think straight. He reached for her again.

"Erin, don't—"

She pushed past him, sprinting across the grass and out to the sidewalk.

He stared after her, some little thread of clarity returning.

What had he just done?

Pick up UNFORGETTABLE by Samantha Hunter, available December 17 wherever you buy Harlequin® Blaze® books.

Your "Dating Boot Camp" Itinerary...

Day One
Fly to a luxurious resort in St. Bart's with your personalized dating coach, Elisa Henderson. Show up on the plane with a guy you just picked up. Find out Brett Jordan isn't just a drool-worthy hottie—he's also a total player...and Elisa's former best friend!

Day Two
Be problematic. Disappear with a cute paparazzo. Besides, Elisa and Brett are now alone in paradise, and Elisa's about to break the first commandment of date coaching: Thou Shall Not Sexily Ravage Your Client's Date. Lost clients, naughty nighttime shenanigans, sleazy paparazzi... Can Elisa avoid tarnishing her reputation?

Pick up
Still So Hot!
by *Serena Bell,*
available January 2014 wherever you buy Harlequin Blaze books.

Red-Hot Reads
www.Harlequin.com

Love the Harlequin book you just read?

Your opinion matters.

Review this book on your favorite
book site, review site, blog or your own
social media properties and share
your opinion with other readers!

Be sure to connect with us at:
Harlequin.com/Newsletters
Facebook.com/HarlequinBooks
Twitter.com/HarlequinBooks

HARLEQUIN®

A *Romance* FOR EVERY MOOD™

Stay up-to-date on all your
romance-reading news with the
Harlequin Shopping Guide,
featuring bestselling authors, exciting new
miniseries, books to watch and more!

The newest issue will be delivered right to you
with our compliments! There are 4 each year.

Signing up is easy.

EMAIL

ShoppingGuide@Harlequin.ca

WRITE TO US

HARLEQUIN BOOKS
Attention: Customer Service Department
P.O. Box 9057, Buffalo, NY 14269-9057

OR PHONE

1-800-873-8635 in the United States
1-888-343-9777 in Canada

Please allow 4-6 weeks for delivery of the first issue by mail.